Money Desires

and

Regrets

D1600900

Jimmy DaSaint

Published By:

PO Box 97
Bala Cynwyd, PA 19004

Website: www.dasaintentertainment.com

Email: dasaintent@gmail.com

ISBN: 978-0-9823111-4-1

Cover Concept and Design by:

Mr. Designer

"This book is dedicated to every man and woman who lost his or her life on the cruel ghetto streets. And to all of us who survive but are slowly dying inside..."

Jimmy DaSaint

"I was a young man on a confused journey.
Lost inside of my own world.
Mislead to a glamorous path that never existed.
A child of the ghetto who grew up to be a man with no
vision. And no presence.
Outside, my world appeared sunny,
but inside my heart was full with pouring
rain. The only love I ever knew were the
streets, until it divorced me, leaving me all
alone.
I became a victim in my own savage game.
Untamed, until I was forced into locks and
chains. But never will I cry.

Everyday is now a
blessing. By losing, a
winner I became
It took me a long time to see it when all I had to do was
just open up my eyes."

Jimmy DaSaint

Chapter One

It was 1994...

. . . And I still can remember the first day I met Chico. I could never forget the scared look on his face when the correction officer first brought him into the joint.

Looking at the small, timid guy made me feel kind of sad for him. I knew that the hawks and vultures would soon be swarming around this new piece of *virgin* flesh; the same men who eagerly waited everyday for fresh meat to be brought through those solid steel bars. I knew Camp Hill Penitentiary was no place for this young man to be, only eighteen and 3000 miles away from home, with no friends or family. He was a rape case waiting to happen.

I had seen it so many times. A young boy comes in, looking forward to becoming a man. But eventually he becomes someone's *girlfriend*, or even someone's *wife*. The sad part about it was, this was just life. And if you weren't able to protect yourself, or fight off these human predators, life was going to be real *fucked* up.

Seeing Chico, reminded me of myself three years earlier, when I was that same timid young man, scared to death in a world I knew nothing about. Luckily, my Uncle Paul was here with me to keep the hawks and vultures far away.

Everyone was afraid of my Uncle Paul, but who wouldn't be of a man standing six-five, weighing three hundred and twenty-five pounds and all muscle. Maybe it was the tattoo on his neck that read *Ready 2 Die*. Whatever it was, it worked. Even after he was released in '93, no one ever fucked with me. After breaking a man's ribs for throwing a basketball at my face, he made it loud and clear; *anybody who fucks with my nephew will suffer the consequences*. So after he left, I was still treated like he was right here inside the joint with me.

From day one, my Uncle Paul taught me the ropes and the rules, how to free your mind and just do your time. He would always tell me there were three important things—mind your own business, stay out of other people's business, and never walk with my head down.

I remember...

The yard was packed on this beautiful spring day. Everyone was on the basketball court playing a game of Ruffhouse 21. The game was so physical that three people were sent to medical. One for a broken ankle, another one for bruised ribs, and the third, after getting sucker punched and knocked out! That's what happens when you keep running your mouth on the court.

Basketball was my game. I was only five-ten, but I could score on anybody. And my jump shot was no joke. You catch me in one of those zones, I might make ten straight, no bullshit! And they all would touch nothing but the bottom of the net.

As the guys and I were playing this wild and reckless game of Ruffhouse-21, I noticed Chico sitting alone on the bench with his eyes on us, but I could tell his mind was miles away.

After making three all-net jump shots, I was only two points away from winning my second straight game. Standing at the top of the key, all I needed to do now was make two free throws to seal the victory. All the guys stood around knowing that these two shots were automatic money in the bank.

I bounced the ball twice before I shot. I looked over at Chico, who now had two guys standing in front of him talking. So I paid it no mind. *Swish*, all net the first shot went.

Half the guys started leaving. One thing for sure, and everyone knew, I wasn't missing no game winning shot from the free throw line.

Looking over at Chico again, I noticed another guy walking up. Now three guys were all standing around him. "Shoot the ball, *nigga*, what are you waiting for?"

"Hurry up," one of the guys shouted. I bounced the basketball two times again and in the middle of shooting this final jump shot to win the game, I stopped! Just like that, I stopped. Looking over at the bench, I saw Chico's face and in his light brown eyes, I could see a fear that I would wish on no man. A look of fright, alarm, panic, and terror, all wrapped up in one.

To this day, I still don't know what made me just drop the ball on the ground and walk over to that bench. Breaking my uncle's first rule—*to mind your own business.*

"What's *going* on?" I said, walking over to the bench.

"Ain't nothing. We were just talking to shorty, that's all," Rock said, looking at me with an expression on his dark-skinned face like, "Why the fuck would I care what was going on." This was the first time that Rock had spoken to me since my Uncle Paul broke his ribs for throwing that ball at my face a few years ago.

"Yeah, we're just chilling, getting to know sweetie, I mean shorty," another one of the guys said as they all burst out laughing.

Looking over at Chico, I could see the uneasiness showing all over his face. And he was not smiling. I wouldn't either if I was sitting around three big black muscular guys who were all planning on fucking me later.

"Well, I'm sorry to burst your bubble, but this is my cousin," I said.

"What! Yeah, *right!*" Rock said, as his laughs quickly turned to frowns with everyone else's.

"Oh, he's *family?*" a voice asked.

"Yeah, he's my peoples," I said, wiping the sweat off my forehead.

"Why didn't you say something," one of the men said.

"I thought you knew. He was over here waiting on the bench for me."

"Sorry 'bout that, little man, we were just playing," the guy said, walking away.

As the other guy quickly followed him, Rock remained.

"What's up, Rock?" I said, taking a seat next to the frightened kid on the bench.

"Cousins, huh?" Rock said, in an angry voice. "Your peoples, huh?"

"Yeah, this is my little cousin, Uncle Paul's stepson," I said.

I guess Uncle Paul's name was all Rock had to hear because he just gave us both this evil look, turned around and walked away.

"Thank you so much," the still frightened young man said.

"Don't worry about it, shorty. You just watch yourself and keep an eye on Rock. He likes turning boys into girls. What's your name?" I asked.

"Rubin Chicarro, but everyone just calls me Chico. What's yours," he asked.

"Jordan Henderson. But everyone calls me Jordan."

"Jordan!" he said, "Like Mike, number twenty-three, Chicago."

"Yeah. Where're you from?"

"L.A. Los Angeles."

"What are you doing locked up all the way in Pennsylvania?"

"Long story."

"How much time you got, Chico?"

"Two to four."

"Well, I got time." I said, folding my arms waiting.

He looked at me for a second, took a long and deep breath, then he began.

"I came out here for my older brother, Pedro. Every two weeks I would bring 5 kilos of coke hidden safely inside my luggage on the Greyhound bus. I would meet our buyer at the Scranton, Pennsylvania bus terminal he would buy all five of the kilos of cocaine at $20,000 a piece. It was always the same thing—5 kilos for $100,000. That was $200,000 a month, $10,000 was mine for every trip I made—*ten thousand bucks*. The buyer was a friend of my brother from L.A. who had moved out here on the east coast to expand his business. L.A. was too competitive,' he said. He probably could have gotten them cheaper himself, but he trusted no one but my brother Pedro. If I didn't take the risk of bringing them on the bus, way across the country, they would have been much cheaper. The last time I met with him, I had 5 kilos and a small .25 automatic that I would always carry. After Valdez received his drugs and paid me the money, he dropped me back at the bus terminal in Scranton, Pennsylvania that was just a few miles away from his home. Once my bus arrived, I took a seat in the back like I had done many times before.

"After all the passengers were on board, the bus still remained in the station. When I looked out the window, I saw the bus driver talking to two men. At first I paid it no mind, but after all three of them walked on the bus, I knew something was wrong. I could just feel it.

"Both men walked past everyone, but stopped at me. 'What is your name?' one of the men said.

'My name is Rubin,' I said, 'Rubin Chicarro,' realizing that these guys were plain clothes cops.

'Do you have any identification?' he said.

'Yes sir,' I said, pulling out my Los Angeles driver's license. After looking at my license very closely to make sure it was me, he finally gave it back. 'We've been having a problem with drugs coming through this bus terminal,' he said. 'Do you mind if we bring in our drug sniffing dog? We received information that there was going to be a major delivery this evening and we've been searching every bus.'

'No, not at all,' I said.

I was prepared for this moment. My brother had schooled me on everything way before my first delivery. Once I would meet the buyer, Valdez, he would take me to his home to take a shower and change into a new set of clothes. Everything I was wearing would be thrown away. Valdez would always have a brand new, different colored backpack. So we were very much prepared for any cops or even sniffing dogs.

"The officer returned with the dog and for about five minutes the dog sniffed around me and my area, as all the passengers just waited and watched. Then the dog walked back and sat by his leg. "As I got ready to take my seat, he interrupted me again. 'One more thing,' he said. 'Do you mind if I check your backpack?'

I paused for a brief second and said nothing. How could I get around this question, I wondered. This was definitely a *trick* question. If I said yes, I'm booked, and if I said no, they would make me wait until they had the proper search warrants to check my backpack. And the result would still be the same...I'm booked.

"So I cut through all the bullshit. I knew they had me, and they knew they had me too. 'I would like to talk to my lawyer,' is what I said, handing over my backpack, filled with $100,000 dollars in drug money, and an unloaded .25 automatic handgun also inside. Luckily, I had emptied out the bullets at Valdez' house. Things could have been worse. After I was read my rights, I was taken to the local county jail. Once I was given my free phone call, I immediately called my brother.

"The next day, he had flown out here to Pennsylvania to post my bail. To our surprise, my bail was denied. After Pedro had gotten me a lawyer to fight my case, he stayed at Valdez' house until the beginning of my trial. My brother felt as though he was the blame for me getting arrested. I was being charged with possession of an illegal firearm, the money was confiscated after I told them that I had found it inside the bus terminal's bathroom. 'Cause I couldn't explain why I was carrying $100,000 in cash inside a backpack. For two months, I was locked up in the county jail. Before my trial was to begin, my lawyer came back with a deal from the prosecutor. The deal was for two to four years. He said it was a chance that they were considering turning the case over to the feds. This really scared my brother and Valdez. After the three of us met, Pedro, Valdez and I all talked. Then I decided to just accept the offer from the prosecutor and do the two to four years. My brother told me to be strong, that once I returned home in a few years, everything would be okay, and I believed him. It's always been him and I. My mother died five years ago and my father abandoned us ever since we moved here from Mexico twenty years ago. My brother has been like my guardian since my mother passed. He's twenty-two years old and it's killing him that I'm here. But there's nothing he can do but wait for at least two more years."

Chico and I continued to talk for the rest of that day. The more he talked, the more I was impressed with his street wisdom. I definitely had Chico all wrong. He had big plans once he got out. He even made me an offer that if I looked out for him, he would look out for me. I figured I could keep the vultures off his back for two petty years. So after this day, that was our deal. I would make sure no one fucked with him, and get him back home safe to his brother. And he would make sure I would never need a dime.

After all, I was getting released a year after him anyway. He would help these two years fly by fast, like the first three did when my Uncle Paul was here. I still think about the six years the judge gave me for that stolen car. I thought I deserved probation, but seeing all of the first-time offenders that were coming in the system, I realized that this country was really serious with its national Hard on Crime campaign. And just like myself a few years ago, Chico was a victim now. Another young man caught up in the fast life of the streets, doing the only thing he was taught to do...*hustle*.

Chapter 2

1995, a year later...

I kept my word and made sure no one bothered Chico. And he also kept his word, making sure every week a hundred dollars was sent to my books from his brother, Pedro, in L.A. After awhile, we became so close I told him that I wouldn't take any more money from him or his brother. Our friendship had blossomed and no amount of money in the world could come between us. No one should have to pay for someone to be their friend, not even me.

All year long, the two of us were inseparable. We worked out in the weight room for three hours every day. After a while, he was no longer that puny lil' five-seven, one hundred and thirty-five pounds timid half-black, half-Mexican kid from L.A. It even surprised me how fast he had grown. In less than eight months, he was standing five-ten, one hundred and sixty-five pounds, staring me straight in the eyes. Everything my Uncle Paul taught me about jail and life, I showed Chico. And he learned every single thing very fast. Nothing seemed difficult for him to master. After I showed him the game of chess in just three weeks he was beating me every time. And he was also good at basketball, but he still had a long way to go before he could ever whip me in B-ball. That was my game and my name wasn't Jordan for nothing! We even had a scheme we would play on other inmates. Chico would bet on me, a best two out of three series. I would lose the first game on purpose then win the second one by a point or two. On the last game, he would bet everything. That's when I would just *blow* the person right off the court. After a while, everyone got hip and stopped playing me. But still, we would always get the new inmates who just came in, thinking they could play ball.

Chico was a nice looking young man with looks like a model. Once he was released back into the real world the women would all be going crazy over him. His dark, black, short, curly hair would certainly drive all the women wild. He told me he had only been with one girl in his entire life. We used to talk about all the different women we would have sex with once we got out. Sometimes I would pick with him and remind him how he almost became a woman. He hated when I did that. But sex, money and basketball were all we talked about. The two of us had built an unbreakable bond. In our own crazy kind of way, we had become brothers.

One day, the two of us were inside the weight room working out when Rock and a few of his friends walked in. Rock was still very upset with me about the whole Chico situation, and my Uncle Paul's as well. On his face I could see in his dark eyes that he had just become fed up. He wanted to *fuck* me up, but most of all, he wanted to *fuck* Chico.

While Chico and I were working out in the corner of the weight room, Rock and his buddies approached us. Everyone inside the weight room immediately stopped what they were doing and began gathering around.

"What's up?" I said, standing in front of Chico.

"I'm *sick* and tired of y'all," Rock said.

"Yeah, well, you know what, Rock, I'm kind of sick and tired of you too," I said, looking him dead in his eyes.

"Well, there's only one way to settle it," Rock said, cracking his knuckles.

"Me and you Jordan, and *when* I knock you the fuck out, the *bitch* is mine," Rock said, as everyone stood around laughing.

"Fuck you Rock! You the bitch mother fucker!" Chico yelled out. "If this is about me, then I'll fight you."

"Nah Chico, I've got this chump," I said, bending down tying up my boots.

"No, Jordan. I'm nobody's *bitch*. I'm tired of this guy and the way he stares at me and blows me kisses. I would never become a man if all I do is run behind you," Chico said, stepping in front of me.

"No, he's too big for you," I said, standing up.

"I don't care. If I lose, at least he'll respect me," Chico said.

"No, *when* you lose bitch, I'm going to *fuck* you," Rock said. "Go watch the door." Rock told one of the guys who was standing next to him.

The crowd quickly formed a circle.

"The coast is clear, ain't no cops around," the man who stood by the door yelled out.

"So who is it going to be, Mr. Basketball or Ms. California?" Rock said, standing in the middle of the floor.

"I got this, Chico. I can take him. He doesn't scare me," I said.

"No Jordan. I'll be all right. I've got to do it or I will never respect myself," Chico said.

I'd never seen him with such a serious look on his face.

Everyone was amazed when Chico stepped up and into the middle of the hardwood floor. All of the weights and benches had been moved out of the way.

Rock was six feet, two hundred and twenty pounds of muscle. After Paul was released, Rock had become the jailhouse bully, extorting money and beating up people. Mostly, taking advantage of young boys who had just come in from the streets. Everyone was afraid of Rock—everyone except me. Chico was terrified of Rock, but today he would have to face his deepest fears. And all six-feet, two hundred and twenty pounds of it stood right in front of him.

Chico had put up his hands like I had shown him, from many nights of shadow boxing together and sparring.

Rock laughed as he swung a wild right hand at Chico's head.

Ducking, Chico quickly hit Rock with a two-punch combination to his body and head.

"Is that it? Is that what you're working with?" Rock said, shaking it off.

The crowd began to get a little louder as the two men circled around each other.

Rock slowly stalked him like a lion hunting for its prey. With his head down, Rock ran at Chico to try and slam him. As Chico moved out of the way, Rock fell on the floor.

Chico stood back as an embarrassed Rock quickly got up. "I'm gonna break your fuckin' neck, *bitch*," Rock said, running at Chico once again.

As Chico ducked, the right uppercut that he threw landed solid on Rock's unprotected jaw. A dazed Rock still remained standing. Throwing a wild left hook, Rock caught Chico right over his right eye. The blow sent Chico to the ground.

Chico's right eye instantly swelled up from the hard blow. I looked at Chico and walked up closer.

"I'm alright," he yelled seeing the concerned look on my face.

As Chico stood up half dazed, Rock ran at him again like a hungry linebacker attacking an unprotected quarterback. The lightning fast Chico then threw another solid right hook to the mouth of the raging bull. The force of the blow knocked the front teeth straight out of Rock's mouth as the blood began pouring from his now busted lip.

The crowd stood around stung, seeing the big bad Rock fall to his knees. As the dazed Rock looked at the blood running from his mouth in disbelief, Chico threw a powerful right kick, hitting Rock on the side of his head, knocking him out cold.

Instantly, the once hostile crowd became quiet. Chico then stood over Rock, grabbing his head by his short dreads. "Who's the bitch?" he yelled out.

A dazed and confused Rock said nothing.

With his free hand, Chico punched him again in his bloody face. "Who's the bitch, I said? Who's the bitch now?" Chico yelled again.

"That's enough, Chico, let's go," I said. "You won. He's finished."

"No, Jordan, No, not until he says it," Chico yelled out in an angered voice.

"Who's the bitch?" Chico said, balling his fist up ready to hit Rock again. "This is the last time or I'm going to kill you, mother fucker. Who is the bitch now?"

"I am," Rock struggled to say.

"What? What did you say?" Chico said, with Rock's dreads still in his hand.

"I am ... I'm the bitch," Rock said with blood all over his face.

Slamming Rock's head to the ground, Chico stood up. "Any one of y'all cowards want a piece of me then come on now," he yelled out at the shocked crowd of spectators. But no one said a word. Everyone had just witnessed the beating Rock had gotten. No one wanted the same results.

"If this is y'all hero," Chico said, standing over Rock's body, "then y'all need to find another one because now he's a has been." Rock was lying on the ground with his face in his own blood.

It was September 5, 1995, a day that I will never forget. The day the timid kid from L.A. became a man in PA. From that day on, neither of us ever had another problem with Rock or any of his crew. In fact, Rock had requested and gotten a transfer to another prison to escape the embarrassment of the brutal beating he had taken.

Everyone was surprised that day, including myself. I knew Chico could fight from practicing and training with him, but not even I expected the outcome of his fight with Rock. But, just like David beat Goliath, Chico had beaten Rock. It's funny how history repeats itself, but like they say, what comes around goes around.

August 9, 1996...

This was a sad day for me. It was Chico's final day in prison after serving his two years. He was now twenty-years old, six feet, one hundred and ninety pounds. Even I didn't believe that this was the same kid that I had taken under my wing just two short years ago. But it was.

In my cell that morning, the two of us sat on my bed talking. I wasn't the emotional type, but today I could have cried a million tears knowing he was leaving and I would still be here for another year.

"So you're going back to L.A.?" I said with my head facing the floor.

"Yeah, my brother will be waiting for me."

"I'll miss you, buddy. You be safe."

"I'll miss you too, Jordan. I'll never forget you. I would have never survived in here if not for you, Jordan. I could never forget that I owe you my life."

"Chico, you owe me nothing. I did for you what my uncle did for me, that's all. Maybe one day you'll do the same for someone else."

"I promise I will never forget you and I mean it. Whatever I earn with my brother, I promise I'll give you half. We will meet again."

"Don't promise that, I enjoyed your friendship, but we both knew there would come a day that you would have to go. You owe me nothing."

"How could you say that? You don't know what will happen to you or me," Chico said.

"Today, my friend is the day that the two of us just go our separate ways. I will always have love for you, but so many promises have been broken in my life, and I don't want yours to be another one," I said.

With a tear rolling from his eye, Chico looked me straight in the face. "Thank you. Thank you for everything, my brother."

"You're welcome," I said, as the two of us stood up and gave each other a hug. Sitting back on my cot, Chico walked away and never turned back.

A month after Chico left, I received a letter and a money order for $500. In the letter, Chico said that things were going well with him and his brother, Pedro. He said that once I was released, they wanted me to come to California. I had never been to California—I was a Philly boy. I knew nothing about the west coast and I never had any interest in going. Still, the offer was nice. I wrote Chico back telling him thanks for the invitation, but I'm cool.

I guess he was determined to change my mind, because every other month after that I would receive another letter with a $500 money order inside asking me to come out to L.A. Even though his offer would always sound good, I missed Philadelphia—the Sixers, Eagles, Flyers, soft pretzels and cheese steaks. I couldn't wait to get back to West Philly, though L.A. sounded like the perfect place.

There was no place in the world like Philly. Philly was home. But more importantly, I had missed my seven-year-old son whom I had only seen once in my life. Even though his mother left me once I came to prison, my son, Marquise, was still my responsibility and I had to get back to Marquise before these streets beat me to him—the *deadly* streets of Philadelphia.

Chapter 3

1997, a year later...

Walking through the thick prison gates, I saw my mother and younger brother sitting inside her old '88 Buick Regal! Seeing me walk down this path to freedom they quickly got out of the car. "Jordan!, Jordan!," my brother Shawn said running towards me.

"I missed you Jordan," he said.

"I missed you too, Shawn," I said, and gave him a big hug.

"Man you grew up fast."

"I'm fourteen now," he said.

The last time I had seen Shawn he was barely four feet high, now my little brother was steering me straight in the eyes. Looking at my mom, I could see the few gray streaks of hair growing in through her dark wavy hair. My mother was just forty-three, but even with the gray hair, she still didn't look a day over thirty-five. With a flood of tears running down her face she wrapped her arms around.

"Are you okay baby?" she said, as I remained clutched tightly in her loving arms.

"Yes mom I'm okay," I said, as a tear ran down from my

face.

"I missed you so much Jordan, I'm so glad its all over with now."

"I know mom ... I know," I said, reaching over and grabbing Shawn who stood there in tears.

"It was so hard not having you around Jordan," My mother said.

"Well, I'm back now, and I don't plan on ever leaving y'all again."

For six years, this was the day that I had been waiting for, but it was also the day that I had feared. With only a GED and $2500 that I saved from the money orders from Chico, I had to once again face one of my biggest fears—surviving the streets.

My mother was working two jobs to pay for my brother's education at St. Elizabeth Catholic School in West Philly. She figured she had lost one son to the *evil* streets; she was not going to lose another one. And after talking with my brother, Shawn, I realized that he was indeed a very bright kid. At least one of Mom's kids would be somebody.

A month later...

I slept on the living room couch in Mom's two-bedroom apartment. I knew I couldn't take this for long, but for now, this had to do. Everyday I would go looking for a job, always getting the same answers, don't call us, we'll call you.

On the kitchen table I had a stack of newspapers that I had searched through looking for a job to help out my tired mother. For hours I would sit and go through each paper, circling certain job possibilities. In less than a month I had filled out over a hundred job applications and no one had called me back. But still I was determined to live the American life, and work a legal nine to five job, paying bills, and taxes. But the more I was denied, I knew no one wanted to hire an ex-con with nothing but a lousy GED I was fooling myself. After giving my mother $1500 to help with the bills for a few months, I was down to my last thousand bucks. Now I had to do something and *real* soon.

Two days later... while looking for a job I ran into a friend of Cookie's, my son Marquise's mother. After getting her address from the friend, I got into my mom's old Buick and drove to Seventeenth and Lehigh in North Philly where Cookie was now living with her grandmother. I noticed the old looking two-story row house and pulled into an empty space. After parking the car, I got out and walked to the door. Upon knocking on the solid wooden door, I stood and waited. A few moments later... the door opened. Standing there with a pair of dirty blue jeans shorts, a dingy wrinkled white T-shirt, my son, Marquise, had no idea who I was.

"You want my mommy, mister?" he said, in the sweetest kid voice.

For a moment I was silent, as I looked at how big my beautiful child had grown. His dark curly hair was all over his face. His light brown complexion was a shade lighter than mine, but everything else was almost identical, his eyes, nose, ears. *This was definitely my junior, Jordan Marquise Henderson junior. A smaller version of me*, I thought to myself.

"Yes. Can you go get your mother?" I asked.

"Okay, wait right here. My grand mom don't like a lot of boys in her house," he said running back inside.

"Mommy, a man wants you at the door," I heard him yell.

"Is it Steve?" I could hear her saying in the background.

"No, another man, Mommy, another man," Marquise yelled.

"Okay, tell him I will be there in a minute," she said.

Marquise quickly ran back to the door. "She's on her way, mister. What's your name?" he asked.

"Before I could open my mouth, Cookie came to the door. Standing there in a large white robe, our eyes finally met again after six long years of separation.

"Go inside, Marquise, hurry up," she said.

"But Mom…"

"Go now, I said."

Marquise put his head down and walked back inside.

"How did you find out where I live, Jordan?" Cookie asked, standing in the doorway looking like a lost crack fiend. As she nervously stood there scratching the back of her neck, licking around her dry lips, I knew I was right. She was on drugs. And bad.

"It doesn't matter. What happened to you, Cookie?" I said staring at her tired reddish eyes. She looked like she hadn't been to sleep in weeks. "Girl, how could you let yourself be like this?"

"Jordan, don't come around here trying to put your foot down after leaving me six years ago."

"I didn't leave you. I went to *prison*."

"You left me. You left me with *nothing*. *Nothing* but your son to take care of, and now you want to come back like ain't shit wrong. Everything got fucked up when you left," she said, crying. "*Everything*."

"I'm sorry if this is not what you expected, but this *is* life. Cookie, you were beautiful," I said.

"What is beauty, Jordan? The only thing that beauty does for a woman in the ghetto is get her rent paid. I have a son, your son. I did what I had to do for us because you were not around because you left us."

"I went to *jail*."

"Whatever," she said. "Whatever, Jordan."

"When I was home, you didn't need anything. Every time I would steal a car and sell it, I would bring the money home."

"Jordan, that was then, six years ago. What was I supposed to do, steal cars too? I was sixteen years old and pregnant."

"Why did you stop coming to see me?"

"I was tired of seeing you behind those bars. Six years sounded like a lifetime; I could no longer take it."

A green Lexus ES300 pulled up in front of the house. A full-bearded, brown-skinned man shouted from in the car. "What's up, Cookie? You ready to see me?" he said, turning down his loud car radio.

"No. No, not right now, Steve, come back later," she said.

Rolling up his car window, he just pulled off.

"Is that your man or *something*?" I asked.

"No, he's just a friend, that's all," she said, looking as the car turned the corner.

"Who is *he*?"

"Jordan, it's none of your business."

"That's who you get your drugs from, huh?"

"What?"

"What do you think I am, stupid? You don't think I know what's going on? Look at you. What happened to your long hair? Look how skinny you got. You barely weigh a hundred pounds. You are nothing but a *fucking* crackhead!"

"Fuck you, Jordan, it's all your fault."

"No. No. No, you can't blame this *shit* on me. I might have gotten locked up and was taken away from you and my son, but I didn't put any pipe in your hand. That was all you."

"I *hate* you. You don't know how much I *hate* you."

"No, Cookie. You hate the *truth*," I said. "You hate the *fuckin'* truth."

"Jordan, what do you want? What did you come here for?"

"My son. I came for Marquise."

"What! Marquise doesn't even know you."

"I want to take him to live with my mother. I'll make sure he's taken care of. Please, Cookie, let me take Marquise with me."

"Jordan, he's *my* baby," she cried.

"Look at you, Cookie. There's nothing you could do for him until you take care of yourself first. You need help. I'll help you get your life straight, I promise, but Marquise is our child. He cannot be around this environment any longer. Your grandmother is old and you're on drugs. At least give our son a chance. I'm back now. I will make sure he becomes somebody."

"Jordan, he's *all* I have," Cookie cried.

"He will just be living with my mother. Whenever you want to see him, he will be there and you can always come visit."

"Jordan, I *love* that boy."

"Then show your love, Cookie, and let me raise him right. At least until you're able to be a responsible mother again."

"Okay Jordan, I'll let him go with you for a little while, because he should know his father, something I never had in my life," Cookie said.

"Thank you Cookie, all I ask of you is a chance to be a father to my son, you know that I would never do anything to hurt our child. Even though he don't know me yet, Marquise means the world to me."

"Jordan I do need a small favor," Cookie said.

"And what's that?"

"I need some money, Jordan."

"What? What did you say?"

"You heard me. I need some money. I need some money now. If you give me a thousand dollars I promise I won't ask you for another dime and I won't bother you again. Never."

I couldn't believe the words that I just heard. But Cookie was serious. Though I knew it was the drugs speaking, I played on. I just wanted my son.

I reached into my pocket and pulled out the $500 I had. "This is all I've got," I said.

"How much is that?" she asked.

"Five hundred bucks."

"I'll take it," she said, snatching it from my hand. "Wait right here," she said as she quickly walked inside.

As I waited outside, I took a seat on the steps. Thinking to myself how this once beautiful woman was now a strung-out crackhead.

Marquise was watching cartoons when Cookie sat next to him on the couch.

"Hey, little man, you're watching your Flintstones, huh?"

"Yes, Mom," he said, looking into his mother's tearful eyes.

"I want you to meet somebody, Marquise."

"My dad?" he said.

"How did you know?"

"I heard y'all talking. I was behind the door listening at first."

"What did I tell you about listening to grown folks' conversations?"

"I'm sorry, Mom, but I never saw him before and I didn't want another man hitting on you like Steve, so I grabbed my bat."

"Oh, you were protecting me?" Cookie said smiling.

"Yes, Mom. When I grow up, I'm going to beat up all those bad men who hit you, especially Steve."

"Thank you, my little soldier," Cookie said, hugging him.

"Your father is not a bad man."

"I know. He went to jail, I heard him say it. I heard him say he wants to take me away. Mom, please *don't* let me go. Please, Mom. I'll be good, I promise, Mom. I'll start cleaning up my room. Please, Mom, don't let him take me."

"Baby, you need to know your father and you need to go to school. I will come see you every week, I promise."

"Mom, I don't want to leave you. I don't want to go."

"Marquise, I will be right here. Whenever you want to talk to me, you can call. Your father is a good man. Please, will you go with him, for me, for just a little while, till Mommy gets us a nice house to live in? One with a big room and a nice color TV to watch the Flintstones."

Looking at the flow of tears rolling down his mother's face, Marquise agreed. "Okay, mommy. I'll go. Stop crying," he said, hugging his mother. Standing up, the two went upstairs to Marquise's room to pack his clothes.

After gathering up some clothes and a few toys, Marquise and Cookie walked into the front bedroom. His grandmother was lying on the bed and smiled as they approached.

"Grand mom you woke, Marquise said, holding her hand.

"Hey little fellow, how's my little handsome guy doing?"

she said.

"I'm okay Grand mom," Marquise said.

"What's in the bag?"

"It's my stuff, I'm leaving," Marquise answered.

"Where are you going?"

"He's going away for a while grand mom," Cookie interrupted.

"With who? Where are you taking him?"

"His father, Jordan is home from prison and he wants him for a little while."

"Jordan is home? Has it been six years already?"

"Yes he's outside waiting to take him Grand mom."

"Oh baby I'm gonna miss you. Come here, come give your Grand mom a hug," she said, sitting on the edge of the bed Marquise reached over and hugged his grandmother.

"I'm gonna miss you too Grand mom. Mommy said I'd only be away for a little while."

"And how long will that be Cookie?"

"Just long enough for him to get to know his father, he needs to know Jordan."

"You be good little fellow, and don't get into no trouble."

"I won't. I promise I'll be a good boy." Marquise smiled. "I love you. You make grand mom proud. You hear me?" "I love you too Grand mom, Marquise said, seeing the tears now rolling down her face.

"Come on Marquise, your father is outside waiting for you," Cookie said, grabbing his hand. "Bye-bye Grand mom."

"Bye-bye Marquise," she said, as he and Cookie walked out the room.

I was now standing up as I was waiting outside. A few moments later, Cookie and Marquise came to the door. Marquise was holding a large green trash bag in one hand and a baseball bat in the other.

"I'll take that," I said reaching for the heavy bag.

"No, I got it. I can carry it," Marquise said, walking to the car dragging the bag.

"The door is open," I yelled. "Put it inside."

"Take care of *my* baby, Jordan."

"I will. I know you'll get yourself together, Cookie."

"I'll be alright. I'll call you and check up on him."

"Here's my mother's address and phone number," I said, passing her a piece of paper.

The two of us walked to the car. Marquise was sitting in the passenger seat waiting. He sat in silence with his arms crossed and a hard look on his face.

I got into the car and turned it on. Cookie was talking to Marquise on the other side of the car.

"You be good," she said, kissing him on his cheek.

"I will."

"You listen to your dad, you hear me."

"Yes, Mom."

"I will call you and I will come see you."

"Okay, Mom, don't forget."

"I won't, my little soldier. Remember what I told you."

"I will Mom, see," he said, showing her his eyes.

"Okay, I love you. I will call you later."

"Bye, Mommy, I love you too."

As Cookie backed away from the car, I slowly pulled off. Looking out the window at his mother, Marquise continued to wave goodbye as I drove. I could see the tears rolling down

Cookie's face as she stood in her large bathrobe in the middle of the street. The sight of Cookie standing there hurt me deep down inside, knowing that the hardest thing a mother could ever do is let one of her children go.

"Everything will be okay, Marquise, I promise. You'll like your other grandmother too."

"I have another grandmother?"

"Yes, my mother. And you have an uncle too."

"I do?"

"Yup. He's your Uncle Shawn."

"Is my other grandmother nice?"

"Yes, she is very nice."

"My Grandmamma is sick. She's in a wheelchair now."

"What's wrong with her?"

"She had a stroke, my mommy said. What's a stroke?"

"It's when people get sick and can't do things like they used to anymore."

"That's why my Grandmamma can't cook any more or walk anymore?"

"Yeah, that's why. What did your mommy tell you?" I asked him.

"Huh," Marquise said, wondering what I was talking about.

"When you pointed at your eyes, why did you do that?" I said.

"She told me to never cry. Boys don't cry, only girls."

"She did?"

"Yup. I *never* cry, even when Steve hit me. I never cry."

"Steve *hits* you?"

"Yeah, he smacked me upside my head when I told him to stop hitting my mommy, but I didn't cry."

"Steve always hit on y'all?"

"Not me, but he always hits my mommy. One time he pulled a gun out on her."

"He did?"

"Yup that's why I have my baseball bat. He'll never hit on me again and I'll get him one day for hitting mommy."

"You don't have to worry about Steve ever hitting you again," I said.

"What about mommy?"

"He won't be hitting on your mommy either."

I still can remember the large smile that was Marquise's face when I said those words.

"Can I hit him *too*?" he asked.

"He's too big for you, but Daddy will take care of him," I said, as Marquise remained smiling the whole ride.

And I meant every word. Steve would one day pay for pulling out a gun on Cookie in front of my child.

Chapter 4

A month later...

My mother enrolled Marquise back in school. For him to have been out of school for almost five months was just terrible, he was a very smart child and passed the test to be placed in his right grade.

For two weeks, Cookie called everyday. After that, the phone calls just stopped. When I went by her house one day, a neighbor said she had put her grandmother in a nursing home up in Germantown and he hadn't seen her in days.

Another neighbor said she would stay in the crack house that was around the corner. When I went by there, no one had seen her either in a few days.

Marquise was doing fine. My mother had taken him shopping and bought him some new clothes and a bicycle. It was the first bike he ever had and I had the privilege of teaching him how to ride it.

After getting bunk beds, he and Shawn were now sharing the room together. The two of them quickly became very close.

The next few months, all was fine. I still didn't find a steady job, but Marquise was okay and that's all that mattered. The only sad time was when he would come in from school to watch his favorite Flintstones cartoon. Sitting next to the phone always waiting for his mother to call and always being disappointed, but still, never would he cry.

For the next few days I searched for Cookie everywhere. One day while driving over to her grandmother's house, I was surprised to see the front door and windows boarded up. A neighbor told me that the city had come out and boarded the place up and he had seen Cookie holding a suitcase, getting into a green Lexus with some guy.

Christmas was in a few days and I knew that no gift in the world would bring greater joy to Marquise's little heart than seeing his mother on Christmas morning.

On Christmas Eve, I think I searched the entire North Philadelphia looking for Cookie.

That night...

While driving down Broad Street I noticed a group of women all standing out in the cold at a Sunoco gas station at Broad and Lehigh. As I slowly pulled up, I noticed that one of them was Cookie.

"Cookie, Cookie," I yelled out the car window.

Surprised to see me, she came to the car.

"Jordan, how did you know where I was?"

"That doesn't matter. Just get in," I said as she opened the door and got inside.

"I can't stay long. I'll get in trouble," she said.

"What are you talking about?"

"I'm working tonight. It's Christmas Eve."

"Don't tell me you're selling pussy?"

"I'm working. I've got to pay the bills. Now what's up?"

"Stop lying. Your grand mom's house is boarded up. I went there already."

"How's Marquise?"

"He misses his mother, how do you think," I said.

"I called and no one answered the phone."

"Stop *fuckin'* lying! Marquise waits by the phone everyday. Everyday he waits for you to call."

"I'm sorry, Jordan, I've been busy. Steve needs me."

"Your *son* needs you!" I yelled.

"Here, can you give him this," she said, pulling out a stack of small bills. "It's $187."

"No, you're going to give it to him. You're going to be there tomorrow morning when he wakes up."

"I can't. Steve will be very upset."

"*Fuck* Steve! *Fuck* Steve!" I said, in a loud voice.

"Jordan, Steve is a very dangerous man. I don't want you getting into any trouble. You just came home."

"If you don't leave with me then I will wait right here all fuckin' night for this guy. Our son needs his mother and you *will* be there tomorrow morning."

"Okay, okay, Jordan. Hold on one minute," Cookie said.

"Barbara. Hey, Barbara," Cookie said, calling one of the women who was standing just a few feet away.

A tall, pretty dark-skinned woman walked up to the car.

"What's up, Cookie?"

"I need a favor, Barb. It's very important."

"What? What's wrong?"

"I need you to cover for me."

"For how long?"

"Till tomorrow."

"What! Girl, you know…"

"Barb, please, it's for my son. It's Christmas, please."

"Okay, but it will cost you. I'll tell Steve you're with Sonny. He knows Sonny's a big trick and likes to enjoy himself all night."

"Thank you, Barb. I owe you girl."

"Kiss the little cutie for me," she said walking away.

"I will. Thank you," Cookie said. "Where are we going now?"

"To my mom's house. You've got to clean yourself up. You can take a shower and do something with your hair. But first, we're going to get him a gift with that money you have. I have a few dollars too. I don't want him seeing you looking like this."

Pulling out of the gas station lot, I drove down Broad Street.

A few hours later…

After picking up some things from down South Street, Cookie and I went back to my mom's place. The stores on South Street were still open for the late Christmas Eve shoppers so we were able to get a few things for her and Marquise. Everyone was asleep when we entered late that night. The beautifully decorated Christmas tree lights were blinking and Christmas songs were playing on the radio.

Cookie had bought some new clothes and underwear to put on. I showed her to the bathroom and she went in to freshen up.

I wrapped and placed Marquise's gifts under the tree then sat on the couch and turned on the TV.

Forty-five minutes later...

Cookie walked out of the bathroom, wearing a large white T-shirt and a pair of white shorts. She sat on the couch beside me. For a moment, I got lost in her beauty. She was still a gorgeous woman, all five feet six inches of her. But in my heart I knew she could never be the woman who I had loved just six years ago.

"I wrote you something while you were in the bathroom."

"What is it?" Cookie asked, looking at the paper I held in my hand.

"It's a poem I wrote for you."

"Give it here. Let me read it," she said, snatching it out of my hand. Sitting back on the couch she begin reading the poem to herself.

Your Paradise

Once a woman open up her legs,
she's given away her most precious gift
She will always remember her first.
Someone shall never forget
It's worth more than gold and diamonds combined.
For us it's the beginning of life and time.
Many lustful men will lie just to get it.
Then forget your name after they hit it.
Most women don't even see it, and just say so be it.
But so many end up scorned,
even mentally and emotionally torn.
Crying deep inside, usually from so many regrets.
Realizing that giving it away wasn't worth
the ten minutes of sweat.
Knowing it was only lust and sex,

but was wishing for love and respect.
Now once he has come, he's gone,
and your mind goes into zone.
Will I ever see him again? Will he call me on the phone?
You're so tired of hurting and singing the same song.
But how can you ever blame him, if you made the first wrong?
By givin' away your paradise to a stranger, or an infatuation.
Knowing you could have been so much smarter,
and just a little more patient.
Being inside of you is the closest thing to heaven.
So tell me why so many queens keep inviting in the devil.
For money, jewels, even clothes and cars.
Many will give up her paradise and accept him raw.
Let him abuse you sexually, recklessly,
while on your hands and knees.
Now all he's done is conquered his prey,
while you think about babies and disease.
This pleasure has a devastating effect,
but still most indulge in this sin.
Remember its up to you to give up your paradise,
so make sure its worth it in the end.

After Cookie read the poem she got up and put it inside her coat. Then she sat down on the couch and cried in my arms.

It hurt to look into her beautiful green eyes and see a woman that I thought I could love forever, a woman that I thought I would spend the rest of my life with, a woman who now didn't even understand the meaning of love, a woman who was lost.

That night, the two of us didn't say much. We both knew

that it was all being done for our child, knowing that afterwards, we would both go our separate ways, realizing that what we had was long gone. But our child shouldn't suffer for *our* mistakes. Still together that night, Cookie fell asleep in my arms, the first time I had held her in over six years.

Christmas day...

The next morning Marquise woke up and walked into the living room. "Merry Christmas Marquise," I said.

"Merry Christmas dad," he said, as he begin to unwrap his presents.

"Merry Christmas Marquise," Shawn said, walking in and taking a seat next to Marquise on the floor by the Christmas tree. "Merry Christmas Uncle Shawn," Marquise said. Walking from out the kitchen my mother and Uncle Paul both stood around smiling. "Merry Christmas Marquise," they said in unison. "Merry Christmas grand mom and Uncle Paul," he said, playing with his red fireman truck.

"Do you like your toys Marquise?"

"Yes Daddy I like them all," he said rolling his truck on the carpet. "Did Santa bring you everything you want?" his grandmother asked. After a long pause he answered, "Yes grand mom."

"Are you sure?" I asked. "I have one more present for you Marquise."

"What dad?" he asked, sitting up.

"First, close your eyes and don't peep."

"Okay. I can't see," he said with his hands over his eyes. "Can I open my eyes now, Daddy?" he said almost immediately.

"Not yet." I said as I walked away to open the bathroom

door.

Cookie walked out of the bathroom and sat on the couch next to me.

"Can I open my eyes now, Daddy?" Marquise asked.

"Yes, you can open your eyes."

Taking his hands down and opening his eyes, the sight of his mother sitting in front of him brought the biggest smile to his face. "Mommy! Mommy! Mom, you heard I missed you, Mom," Marquise said getting up, running into his mother's arms.

"I miss you too, my little soldier. Mommy misses you too."

"Mommy I go to a new school. Daddy takes me every morning."

"Good. I'm so proud of you Marquise. Are you being good"?

"Yes, Mommy. I'm going to be a policeman when I grow up and lock up all those bad men."

"I got you something," Cookie said, grabbing a large white bag from behind the couch. "Here, it's from me and your father," she said, passing the bag to Marquise.

Opening up the bag, Marquise smiled as he pulled out the Flintstones pajamas. Reaching inside the bag again, he then pulled out a new pair of white Air Jordan's, then a Guess jeans set.

"That's not all," Cookie said, as the joyful tears ran down her face.

My mother was now standing by the tree watching everything, crying also.

Taking out a small box from the bottom of the bag, Marquise sat in-between Cookie and me.

"What's this, Mom?" he said, holding the box in his hands.

"Open it and see."

A small gold chain lay neatly inside the box.

"Do you see what the piece says?" Cookie said, smiling.

Marquise took the chain from the box and read the small gold pendant that was attached.

"Never Cry," Marquise said, smiling. "It says, *Never Cry*."

Cookie then put it around his neck. "Don't ever take it off."

"I won't, Mommy, thank you. Thank you, Daddy."

"You're welcome, Marquise," we said together.

"I love y'all," he said, hugging both his mother and me.

"We love you too," Cookie said crying.

"Now go open up the rest of your gifts and let me see what else you got."

As Marquise went to open his toys, Cookie and I just stared at each other. Seeing the excitement on our child's face made this Christmas day the best day of both our lives, because today was the first time that we were ever a family.

That night, while everyone was asleep, Cookie wrote a letter and set it on the coffee table before she walked out the door.

Early the next morning, while everyone was still asleep, I sat on the couch and read her letter.

Dear Jordan,

I'm sorry for leaving, but you could never understand how I feel. I realize that Marquise is better off with you and your family. Thank you so much for taking him. I was not a good mother. It hurts, but it's the truth. I'm a failure. I need to get myself togeth-

er. He needs you to help make him a man, something I could never do. I know it hurts him to see me looking this way. That's why I've got to get myself straight. I love you, Jordan. I wish things could have been different between us, but I messed that up. I let these streets destroy me. I used to blame you the whole time. I could have been there for you while you were in prison. Instead I ran. Ran to the streets, losing myself in the process. Maybe one day I'll find myself. Until then, take care of our son and make sure he never cries.

Love, Cookie

After reading Cookie's letter, I sat back on the couch, firmly controlling the tears that wanted to fall from my eyes, asking God to keep Cookie safe from the evils of the streets and the demons that controlled her confused mind.

Chapter 5

February 1998... a few months later...

Uncle Paul had come by to see me. He had a job being a body-guard for different people around the city, rappers, actors, hustlers, whoever needed the service of a six-five, three hundred and twenty-five pound ex-convict. He even offered me a job, but I declined. It just wasn't my thing. After I used up every penny I had, my mom would give me a few dollars for gas to continue looking for a job. No one wanted to hire me and I wasn't working at any McDonald's. Still I tried and still I was denied.

It was actually harder surviving on the streets than inside the pen. At least I didn't have to worry about bills and shit like that. Now, my worries were everything, bills, food, clothes, school, gas all of this with no more money and no job, making me wonder how do these people expect us to survive? First they're locking everybody up and throwing away the key. And once our time is up, we're thrown back to the wolves...the streets.

They're taking out welfare, but bringing in cocaine. Can't get books for our schools, but they can get guns for our neighborhoods. What a country.

I realize that we can't live without these people, because they do not understand us. How can they understand something they don't know? And they can watch all the Spike Lee and John Singleton movies they want. They can read all the Terry McMillan and Eric Jerome Dickey books on the shelf. Still they could never understand us until they have gone through what we've been going through since we were brought to this country over 200 years ago ... *Pain and death.*

I can still remember sitting out front on the porch, watching the expression on Marquise's face as he rode his bike up and down the street. Seeing him so happy would make me sometimes wish that I had known my own father as a child growing up. Shawn and I had different fathers. His father would come get him every other week to give my mom a break. But I never knew my father. I had only seen a few pictures of him. All I know is that my mom would say that he was only good in his whole life for *one* thing—and that was me. So I just left it alone.

That night as I lay on the couch, the telephone rang. "Hello? Who's this calling at one o'clock in the morning?" I asked.

"It's only ten in beautiful L.A.," the voice on the opposite end of the phone said.

"Chico! Chico!"

"Jordan, what's up?"

"I thought you forgot about me after I was released from prison."

"Jordan, I told you that I would never forget you."

"Why didn't you call?"

"I lost your mother's number. I've been looking for

months and finally today I found it and decided to call you, homeboy. I keep my word, I told you that! I was about to fly out to Philly to find you, my brother."

"I thought something happened to you," I said.

"In L.A., no way. This is my city. So how have things been going with you?"

"Not too bad. I don't have a steady job yet, but I'm holding out. You know some interviews and some call backs."

"Come to L.A., Jordan. You'll love it out here."

"I can't. I have to help out my mother and my son."

"Just for a few days. You'll be back before you know it. Come on."

"Chico, right now would be a bad time to leave. His mother ran off. It would kill him if I did the same."

"Bring him, bring him with you."

"I couldn't do that. He's in school."

"Well you need to come to L.A., Jordan. I can't say too much on the phone, but I can promise you this, you will not be disappointed."

"I believe you, but right now, Chico, it's really a bad time."

"I understand, my friend, I do. I have your mother's address and number now. This time I won't lose it. Do you need anything?"

"No, I'm fine," I said.

"I see you're still working with your Philly pride."

"I'm okay. I told you in jail, you don't have to pay for a friend. Money can't buy a real friendship."

"Yeah, but money can pay rent," Chico said.

"I'm fine Chico, I'll be okay"

"Jordan don't get like this on me. Let me help you dawg.

Please."

"But Chico…"

"No buts, Jordan I'm wiring a few dollars tomorrow and that's *that*"!

"Okay Chico, I see you won't take no for an answer."

"That's right."

"Damn! You stubborn man."

"I got it from you," Chico said. "I still want you to think about coming to L.A. you're always welcome. My brother is looking forward to meeting you. He wants to meet the guy who made my bid so easy."

"I'll think about it." I said.

For the next hour, Chico and I just talked about old times. I could tell that he had missed me 'cause I had felt the same. And as much as I wanted to go to L.A., I just couldn't leave Marquise. Nothing was more important to me than him.

The Next Day, at Western Union…

After showing my I.D. and giving my secret code, the lady walked to the back. For a moment, I thought something was wrong as I nervously waited at the thick glass window that stood between us.

Walking back, she sat down on her stool. "How would you like that, sir?" she said, holding a large stack of brand new big-face hundreds.

"It doesn't matter," I said.

Counting out ten one hundred dollar bills, she passed them through to me.

"Holdup, What's all this!" I asked.

"It's your money, sir"

"You sure?"

"I'm positive, sir, your code is Calidelphia, right?"

"Yes, that's it," I said, scratching my head.

"You're the only person we were expecting with the code and I.D. Believe me, it's no mistake."

"How much is it? Never mind, never mind. You can just give it to me."

She counted out another ten brand new hundred-dollar bills and handed it through the window.

"Two thousand bucks, I don't believe Chico," I said smiling.

"That's not all, sir," the lady said, counting out another thousand dollars.

"Oh, shit," I said, shaking my head. "Three thousand dollars!"

"Can you please sign this," the lady said, passing a large white piece of paper and a receipt to me.

After signing the paper, I gave it back.

"This is yours," she said, passing me a piece of paper.

"What's this," I asked.

"It's a message from the sender," she said, pointing to the next person who was waiting in line.

Walking out the door, I unfolded the piece of paper, it read: *Beautiful women, movie stars, fancy cars, and perfect weather. What are you waiting for?*

I just smiled and got into my mother's car. Chico was real persistent and doing a real good job of convincing me to go out to California. But every time I thought about leaving Marquise, my California dream disappeared.

For $2,000, I bought a used car. It was a 1993 red Chevy Corsica. Even though it had over a hundred thousand miles on it, it ran like a beauty. Now I didn't have to use my mother's car anymore. With the remaining $1,000, I gave $500 of it to my mom for Marquise.

After job-hunting for a week, I had finally found some work at a Dunkin' Donuts on Roosevelt Boulevard. Mr. Sanders the manager said he'll give me a chance and wouldn't hold my past against me. One evening, Mr. Sanders, called me, Morlean, a fat white girl from South Philly, and Calvin, a skinny white kid from Roxborough into the back office, just before the next shift was due to come in. As we all stood there, he began speaking.

"We have a problem," he said. "A very serious problem."

"What's wrong, Mr. Sanders?" Morlean asked.

"We have ourselves a thief, and I hate thieves," he said staring at me.

"What's stolen?" Calvin asked.

"Somebody took $100 from the cash register."

Everyone looked around at each other.

"This is a criminal matter. I will definitely notify the police and the person will be immediately fired," he said, pacing the room. "Before I look at this video to see who has been stealing, please do yourself a favor and save yourself the embarrassment now," he said.

No one said a word as the three of us all stood there.

"This is my final chance," he said, still staring at me.

"Okay, then," he said, reaching for the VCR that was sitting on his shelf.

"It was me . . . I did it."

Calvin and I both looked at Morlean.

"I'm sorry, Mr. Sanders, I needed it. I didn't think it would be noticed."

"Morlean, how could you. You've been here for over a

year. You just got employee of the month. Why?"

"I'm sorry, sir, the pay just doesn't help me and my two kids."

"Why didn't you come to me and just ask for some overtime, Morlean?"

"I was desperate. I wasn't thinking straight," she said, crying.

"Can y'all two please leave the room for a minute," Mr. Sanders said to Calvin and me. Walking out I shut the door behind us.

"Damn! Morlean got caught. I told her," Calvin said.

"You knew she was stealing?" I asked.

"Yeah, she's been stealing money ever since you started working here."

"Oh, yeah."

"Yeah. She found out that you were an ex-convict and knew if they found out some money was missing that you would be blamed for it."

"That fat *bitch*!" I said in an upset voice.

"She took some money last week too."

"I knew something was up with her, always wanting to count the money," I said.

"I told her that you were a nice guy trying to get your life straight. She didn't care. She said you probably were planning on robbing the store anyway."

I just stood there shaking my head. It didn't matter. In prison, or even in Dunkin' Donuts, *hate* was everywhere, I thought to myself. Mr. Sanders walked out of his office with Morlean and approached us.

"I'm sorry, gentlemen," he said, unable to look me in my eyes now.

"I'm sorry too," Morlean said.

"Morlean will be suspended for two days without pay for what she's done," Mr. Sanders said, smiling, like he did me a big favor. "Even though she's been a very good employee, stealing cannot be tolerated, so she will no longer be working the cash register," he also said.

At first, I wasn't going to say anything. I was new and I really needed the job. Then, I quickly changed my mind.

"So you're not going to call the cops now, Mr. Sanders?" I said.

"Well, I don't think it's really that big of a deal," he said.

"You said that this was a criminal matter and the person would be fired."

"Morlean has been here a while. After talking to her, I decided that she needed another chance."

"But you were going to call the cops and fire me, if it would have been me," I shouted.

Morlean and Calvin stood there in silence with dumb looks on both their faces.

"Jordan, I thought..."

"I know what you thought. And it's people like you, and her, who keep black people like myself down."

"I don't dislike black people," Mr. Sanders said, as the sweat started to roll down his pale white face.

"I didn't say you did. Once you found out that it wasn't me who stole your money, your attitude changed?"

"I... I..."

"I know why you assumed that it could not be anyone else but me who would take money from the cash register. An ex-convict. It's bad that it's usually people like yourself who are in positions to do right, always abuse their power and do wrong,"

I said.

Taking off my Dunkin' Donut jackets and cap, I threw them at him. "This is what you wanted right, another black man out of a job."

"Hold it, Jordan..." Mr. Sanders said, "Let me explain."

"No, let me tell you something. First of all, it's discrimination, second it's disrespect and I could never work here with you because you're not a man. You're a coward hiding behind a manager's title. You're just as bad as the Ku Klux Klan. Matter of fact, you're *worse* because you hide your hate and smile in my face like everything's okay. Only bad will come to you, maybe not now, but it will come. After today, you will not have to worry about me. I'm a firm believer that things will work themselves out. As far as you and her, a thousand prayers couldn't save your deceitful hearts."

After grabbing my jacket off the rack, I walked away, leaving them all standing there with dumb-ass looks on their faces.

Chapter 6

Life was really beginning to get harder. It seemed like the more I tried, the more *fucked* up things got. I think my mom knew how hard things were too because she would always tell me not to worry, it gets greater later, always bringing a smile to my face, momentarily taking away the deep pain that rested inside my grieving soul.

After I spent my last bit of money, I knew I had to do something fast. I knew if I didn't get money soon that I would end up back in prison, because now my back was up against the wall and the wall was slowly beginning to crumble down. I would watch Marquise as he slept, knowing that I had to do something fast. Inside I was a frustrated man. Frustrated at this country for its evil towards its own people. But I was more upset with myself. I felt like a failure. I felt like a man with no tomorrow and no yesterday. My Uncle Paul had told me so many times to never walk with my head down, but slowly it was leaning towards my feet.

I had to help my mother and Marquise before things got worse. More importantly, I had to help myself before I ended up somewhere worse than prison...*the grave*.

Lying on the couch that night, so many thoughts ran through my troubled head, but as I laid back thinking, my confusion began to clear up. For the first time in a while, I was finally looking forward to tomorrow; because now I knew I had to make a decision. Now I knew what had to be done. The next day, while everyone was gone, I sat on the couch. My mom was at her day job where she would clean mansions out in the suburbs for rich white people. Then at night she would bartend at the Eldorado Inn, a few blocks away from our house. Marquise and Shawn were both in school. Pulling out a piece of paper with Chico's number on it, I reached for the telephone. It was 11:30 a.m. in Philadelphia and 8:30 a.m. in California, but I had to talk to Chico, and I had to talk to him now.

The phone range four times before a man's voice answered.

"Hello," a voice said, picking up the phone.

"Yes, my name is Jordan. Can I speak to Chico?"

"Jordan! Jordan, my man," the voice said.

"Who's this?" I asked.

"It's me, bro, Pedro."

"Who?"

"Pedro, Chico's brother."

"Oh, what's up, my man?"

"Chico's asleep, but I will wake him up. One minute, bro. Chico, Chico, get up. It's your homeboy," I heard Pedro shouting on the phone.

"Who?" Chico said.

"It's your homeboy from Philly. It's Jordan."

"Jordan!" Chico shouted, "Jordan! What's up? Is everything okay?"

"I'm fine, Chico. I was just calling to see how you were doing."

"I'm on top of the world, bro. You need to be here with me. The world is too big for just one man," Chico said, "Did you change your mind? Are you ready to come to California?"

"I'm ready," I said. "I'm ready."

"I will make all the travel arrangements. When will you be ready?"

"Tomorrow. First I have to talk to my mother and my son," I said.

"Okay, everything will be taken care of. Handle your business at home first. Make sure you keep my number with you. It will always get you in contact with me. I'll use American Airlines. Everything will be already paid for when you get to the airport."

"Okay, Chico. I'll see you tomorrow."

"Peace, homeboy. I'm glad you changed your mind. I'll see you tomorrow."

"Bye, Chico," I said, hanging up the phone.

That evening after my mother cooked and everyone had eaten, the two of us sat on her bed inside her room.

"What's wrong, Jordan? What is it that's been on your mind all evening?" she said, looking me in my eyes.

"Mom, remember my friend I told you about from L.A.?"

"Yeah, your friend from prison."

"Yeah, him."

"Why what's wrong"?

"Nothing, my friend wants me to come see him. He's been begging me to visit him."

"Oh, that's wonderful. So why are you so sad?"

"It's in Los Angeles, and I been really thinking hard about it."

"Jordan, you are a grown man and I know a man must do what he has to do. But Marquise will be devastated."

"I know. I will talk with him later, before I tuck him in bed."

As I stood up and began walking out of her room, my mother called me. "Jordan," she said.

"Yes, Mom, what is it?"

"Don't get caught up in the life. Don't get sidetracked. Do what you have to do and stay focused."

"I will, Mom," I said, as I walked out of her room with a big smile on my face.

All my life I could count on my mother. She has always been my strength. Everything about the streets, she taught me, since having me at only fifteen years old. And all the things that only a man could show me, she made sure her younger brother, my Uncle Paul, would teach me.

My mother had lived a fast and hard life herself, growing up in one of the worse sections of the city, North Philadelphia, in the Richard Allen Housing Projects. My Uncle Paul told me that she would set up drug dealers for my father to rob them, back in the day. They were the ghetto's Bonny and Clyde. I was told how she was so fine that every man in the neighborhood wanted her, but she only had eyes for my father.

My Uncle Paul told me that every nigga in the projects feared my father. Any every woman was afraid of my mom. I was told that while she was pregnant with me, my mother and father broke up. After I was born, she had slowed down, leaving my father and North Philadelphia behind her and moving to West Philly with me to begin her new life.

One thing for sure, my mother knew me very well. When she looked at me, I could tell she saw my father. I could see how much she loved him. I could see her deepest fears about me too, that I was a hustler, just like her and my father. But she never tried to change me. She knew I was born to get that money; it just was in my blood.

Ever since I was a young kid growing up, I was on money missions, hustling, stealing, robbing, you name it and I had done it. And through my wrong or rights, my mother had always supported me and never left my side.

Marquise was sitting on his bed doing his homework when I walked into his room and sat beside him.

"What's up, little man?" I said, slapping him five like his best friend would do.

"Hey, Dad, I'm doing my math," he said.

"You have one minute for your dad?" I asked.

Closing his book, he sat back on his bed and folded his arms. "What's up, Dad?" he said, looking me in my eyes.

"You know I love you, right?"

"Yes."

"You know I would never do anything to hurt you, right?"

"Yes, Dad, I know."

"I have something to tell you, Marquise."

"What, Dad? Did I do something wrong?"

"No, you've been a good son, the best in the world."

Marquise smiled. "Then what's wrong, Dad?" he asked.

"I have to go away for a little while."

"Where?"

"To California."

"Where the movie stars live?" he said.

"Yeah, where the movie stars live," I said.

"Dad."

"Yes, Marquise."

"Promise me you'll come back and don't stay away like my mommy did."

"I promise, I'll be back, I promise."

"Okay, Dad, remember now, you promised."

"I love you, Marquise, I love you, my little soldier."

"I love you too, Dad," he said, hugging me. "I'll be a good boy and I *will* listen to Grand mom. Just come back."

"I will, Marquise," I said, hugging him.

"What else?" I said.

"And I will never cry," he said. "I will never cry."

Before I tucked Marquise into bed that night, I reassured him once again that I would return to him in a few days. Looking up at me he finally showed me that beautiful smile of his and said, "I know you'll come back dad I know you would never leave me."

Chapter 7

Los Angeles International Airport...
The temperature was in the high 70s when I stepped off the plane in LA. It was my first time on an airplane, and I was scared to death. Maybe it was from always watching the news and seeing planes crash or get hijacked. But it wasn't as bad as I thought, the ride was actually smooth and I slept for three hours.

Walking up to a payphone, I called the number that Chico had given me. After two rings, he answered.

"What's up, Jordan?"

"Chico, how did you know it was me?" I said.

"I've been watching you the whole time."

"Where are you?" I said, looking around.

"Right in front of your face," he said, laughing.

"Where? Where are you?" I said, still looking around.

"Look in front of you. What do you see?"

"A limo, a cab, and three tinted black CL500 Mercedes. Are you in the limo?"

"Nope."

"The cab?"

"Now you know better."

"Oh, shit! One of those Mercedes?" I said, dropping the phone and walking over to the three-parked Mercedes.

The door to the car in the middle opened up and Chico jumped out. "Jordan! Jordan," he said, walking towards me, giving me a hug.

"Chico! You crazy ass nigga," I said.

Two men then opened the doors and got out of one of the other Mercedes.

"Jordan, this is my brother, Pedro," he said, introducing us. "And this is my homeboy, Sid."

"What's up fellas?" I said, shaking their hands.

"What's up, Jordan? About time we finally met," Pedro said, smiling.

"Yeah, it's about time," I said.

"Thank you, man, for helping my little brother."

"It's nothing. You thanked me enough."

"It's something, you are like family, Jordan. Chico told everyone about you and what you did for him while he was in prison."

"Tonight we are going to celebrate," Chico said.

"Yeah, Jordan, we're going to show you how we party in L.A.," Pedro said.

"Let's roll," Chico said.

I tried to open the door to Chico's car but it was locked "You're not riding with me," he said.

I then walked up to Pedro's car where he and Sid were getting inside. "You're not riding with us either," Pedro said.

"What's up? What's up with y'all L.A. dudes?" I said, looking at Chico and Pedro.

"Here," Chico said, throwing a set of keys at me.

"What's this?" I said.

"It's the keys to your car, stupid," Chico said, pointing to the black CL-500 that was parked behind his.

"My car! What! Chico, no, you didn't."

"Yes, I did. It's yours. The title is in the glove compartment, Mr. Jordan Marquise Henderson."

"Oh, shit! Damn! A CL-500," I said shaking my head in disbelief.

"It's a gift, from Pedro and me, to you," Chico said.

"Damn, you could have just bought me a thank you card," I said.

"It is a thank you card—a thank you card sitting on 20's," Chico said, laughing. "Life has been good. Life has been real good, you'll see," Chico said.

"Are y'all two ready?" Pedro said.

"Yeah," Chico yelled.

"Come on, get in your car and follow us, Jordan."

Walking up to the brand new Mercedes Benz, I still couldn't believe it was mine. I got inside and started it up. The engine purred to life as the electronic dashboard lit up. Damn! A CL-500, I said to myself, looking around inside. Suddenly I heard a phone ring. Looking around, I saw the small grey cell phone on the floor of the car.

"Hello," I said, answering it after the fourth ring.

"You don't like answering your phone?" Chico asked.

"My phone!"

"Yeah, how else are we going to talk," Chico said, laughing.

"What!"

"Your car, your phone, you need both in L.A."

"You are one crazy guy," I said.

"And now, I'm one crazy happy guy because my best

friend is finally here with me."

"Thanks, Chico."

"No, thank you," he said.

"Are y'all two done with the mushy stuff?" Pedro said on the three-way call.

"Yeah. Pedro, let's ride," Chico said.

Pedro then pulled off with me and Chico following him out of the airport. Still, I couldn't believe I was driving my own CL-500 Mercedes Benz, a car that I had always wanted. But not in my wildest dreams, I thought, that I would actually have one.

Philadelphia, Pa., on the corner of Broad and Spring Garden...

"Shut up, bitch!" Steve said, smacking Cookie on the ground. "What did I tell you about my money?"

"I'm sorry, Steve. I don't know what happened to the other $20."

"Bitch! I told you to guard my money with your life."

"I'm sorry, Steve. I'll get it back," Cookie cried.

"How many times do I have to tell y'all whores about fucking up my money," Steve said, looking at the four other women who were standing around. "I make sure y'all have a roof over your head, nice clothes on your back and all the drugs y'all can handle. So why do y'all insist on fucking up bitch Steve's money. Huh? Answer me, goddamit!"

Grabbing Cookie by her hair, Steve pulled out a black Glock 9-millimeter and put it to her mouth. "Bitch, do I have to make an example out of you?"

"No, Steve, no. She didn't mean it," the other girls screamed.

"Shut the fuck up. I'm talking to this slut," Steve said.

"No, Steve, you don't have to make an example out of me."

"Well, if you fuck up my money one more time, you'll be one *dead* bitch. Do you hear me?"

"Yes. Yes, Steve," Cookie said, shaking and crying.

"Any of you bitches," he said, throwing Cookie back to the ground. "Don't let my money get fucked up again," he said, getting into his green Lexus ES300 with a male friend who was inside waiting. Immediately, Steve pulled off and drove down the street.

"That's how you handle those bitches, RW. You got to let them know you ain't no joke," Steve said, as they both started laughing.

Santa Monica, California...

The beautiful house looked like a small mansion from the outside. The house had to cost at least a million dollars or more. Admiring the outside view, I followed Chico and Pedro into a back path that led us to a six-car garage in the back of the house.

I noticed a red Ferrari and a white Porsche parked next to each other as we pulled into the large garage. The large swimming pool and full-length basketball court had also complimented the beautiful backyard scenery.

"Man, this was living," I said to myself. "This was living large."

Getting out of the Mercedes, I continued to look around. The weather was a lot warmer than what I had just left a few hours ago back in Philly.

For that moment, I felt rich. I don't know why, I just did.

"Jordan, come on man, come inside," Chico said, walking

through a small door that was inside of the garage. I quickly followed behind Pedro and Sid.

We all walked through the large kitchen and entered the beautifully decorated living room. A lighted gold chandelier hung from the high ceiling. A large salt-water fish tank was built into the wall with exotic colorful little fish slowly moving around their watery paradise. The soft white leather sofa blended perfectly with the white carpet that ran throughout the living room. All the walls were white too. Only a large picture of a beautiful Spanish woman was hanging.

"Come on, let me show you your room," Chico said, walking up the wide carpeted staircase to a balcony that overlooked the living room.

Following him up the stairs, we entered one of the eight bedrooms that were inside this large exquisite house.

"This is where you'll be staying," Chico said.

Inside the large room I saw an oak brown bedroom set, a king-size bed with a large Sony TV and stereo set up against the wall. This room by itself was almost as big as my mother's whole apartment back in Philly, I thought. The room also had its own bathroom and walk-in closet.

"There are some new clothes I bought for you. Some shorts and T-shirts, socks and underwear inside the closet," Chico said.

"You remember my size, huh," I said, looking at the size of the clothes.

"Extra large, right?" Chico said.

"That's right," I said, taking a seat on the bed.

"We're having a few friends drop by tonight so take a shower and get dressed."

"Who's coming?"

"Friends of ours. People I want you to meet. So you get dressed. I have to make a run with Pedro and Sid. We will be back before you know it."

"Where are you going?"

"We have some business to handle. We'll be right back. If you need anything, just call Ruiz."

"Who's Ruiz?"

"He's our butler, our counselor, our friend, all wrapped in one. His room is at the end of the hall, or just press one on the intercom, and he'll come," Chico said. "He knows about you already, so don't be afraid to call him. I need to talk to you, Jordan, about something real important."

"Go ahead, talk."

"No, not now, later, later after everyone leaves, we will talk," Chico said, walking out of the room and shutting the door behind him.

Reaching in my pocket, I pulled out the cell phone that Chico had given me. I dialed a number and held the phone to my ear until someone answered.

"Hello."

"Mom, what's up?"

"Jordan, is everything okay?"

"Everything is fine, Mom."

"How's California?"

"It's nice, palm trees, freeways and beaches."

"Remember what I told you."

"I will. I won't forget. Where's Marquise?"

"He's sitting right here. Hold on," she said.

"Hello, Dad!"

"Hey, buddy, what's up?"

I did my homework, Uncle Shawn helped me and Grand

mom said after dinner I could ride my bike.

"I love you, Marquise."

"Yes, Dad. I love you too."

"I will be home in a few days, hear?"

"Okay."

"You be good and do what Grand mom says, you hear me?"

"Yes, I will."

"I love you. Now put your grand mom back on."

"Okay," Marquise said.

"Hello."

"Mom, guess what Chico and his brother bought me."

"What?"

"Guess"

"What, you know I don't like guessing things."

"They bought me a brand new Mercedes Benz."

"What!"

"Yeah, mom it's the newest model."

"Chico must really like you."

"Mom, I told you we're like brothers."

"I believe you. Now make sure there aren't any strings attached."

"It's cool, Mom, it's all paid for, title and everything."

"I'm really happy for you, but remember what I told you, to stay focused."

"I will, Mom. I learned from the best."

"I'm glad you are happy. You needed a break from Philadelphia."

"Mom, you should see this house. It's like a mansion, swimming pool, basketball court, it's off the hook."

"Hold on one minute, Shawn wants to talk to you"

"Hey Jordan I miss you already."

"It's only been a few hours since I left."

"I know it just feels strange not seeing you today that's all."

"I miss you too, you make sure you keep a eye on Marquise for me."

"Oh, I will. Me and Marquise stacked all of your newspapers in the closet for you."

"Thanks Shawn, did anyone call me, since I left?"

"No Jordan, no one called."

"Okay. Make sure you help mom around the house and don't forget to keep a eye on your nephew, I love you, now put mom on the phone."

"I love you too. Here mom," Shawn said passing her the telephone.

"So what do you and your friends have planned for tonight?"

"Some people are coming by for me to meet later. Chico had to make a quick run. I'm here alone with the butler."

"The butler?"

"Yeah, his name is Ruiz. I haven't met him yet, but I will later."

"Your friend seems like he's doing good with himself. Maybe your luck will change too."

"Soon as I got off the plane, my luck changed. I'm glad I decided to come out here. Mom, I'm going to call you tomorrow. I have to take a shower and get dressed. Tell Marquise to be good."

"I will. You be safe and don't forget to call us."

"I won't. I'll call tomorrow evening. Bye, Mom."

"Bye, Jordan," my mother said, hanging up the phone.

Laying back I closed my eyes. I then quickly opened them both to see if this was all a wonderful dream. Looking around everything was the same. This was all real. Still I felt as though it was all a big dream.

Chapter 8

After taking a shower and getting dressed, I sat in the living room waiting for Chico and Pedro to come back home. As I was admiring the beautiful fish inside the large tank, Ruiz walked in.

"Do you need anything, sir?" he said, dressed in his black and white butler's outfit.

"No, I'm fine," I said.

Ruiz was a Mexican man who looked to be in his mid 40s. Short and stocky, he walked with a noticeable limp.

"How long have you known Chico and Pedro?"

"I have known the boys all their lives, since they were two bad kids running around on the streets of East Los Angeles. Our families were very close. I love them like they were my own sons. And Chico thinks very highly of you—we all do. We all know what you did for him while he was incarcerated."

"We looked out for each other," I said. "Where are they?"

"The boys will be home soon. They called not too long ago."

"Oh, yeah."

"They're on their way home now. Should be here very

soon. If you need me, I'll be in the kitchen preparing the food for tonight."

"I'm fine, thanks, Ruiz," I said, standing up and walking around the large room.

"There's pretzels and mints over there," Ruiz said, pointing at a glass table in the corner. "I'll be in the kitchen," he said, walking away.

Looking out the large glass window, I thought about Marquise and at the same time, I wondered why it was so important that Chico wanted to talk to me.

An hour later...

Looking out the window, I could see the two Mercedes coming up the driveway. Behind them were a blue Volvo, a white Acura and a silver Lexus.

"They're here," I shouted out to Ruiz as I took a seat back on the sofa.

Ruiz quickly walked to the front door and opened it.

"What's up, Jordan. I see you met Ruiz," Chico said, walking through the door with Pedro.

"Yeah, we met."

Sid then walked through the door with two beautiful Spanish women. "This is my friend, Jordan," Chico said, smiling.

"Hi Jordan, my name is Christion," said the pretty, short bowlegged one.

"And I'm Suzy," the taller one said, showing her beautiful white teeth.

"Nice to meet y'all," I said, shaking both their gorgeous hands. Two more beautiful women suddenly walked through the door.

"This is my friend Jordan, from Philly," Chico said once again.

"Hi, I'm Vennessa," the tall, dark, slim one said, dressed in a tight red dress that fitted perfectly on her body.

"Hi, I'm Kondi," the beautiful short, red bone said, blushing.

"So you're from the city of brotherly love I hear?" she asked.

"Yeah, I'm from Philly," I said, shaking my head.

"Why do they call it the city of brotherly love?" Venessa asked.

"I guess because we brothers have a lot of love to share."

"We have a lot of love to share too," Kondi said, as all the girls stood around giggling.

"Where's Mia?" Pedro asked.

"Right here, calm down, Pedro. I was fixing my hair," she said, walking through the door and shutting it behind her.

Staring at Mia, I couldn't believe how beautiful this woman was. Her light brown eyes complimented her pecan brown complexion. She stood around five-eight, one hundred and thirty-five pounds, with long, black, silky hair laying down her back. This woman was the most attractive woman I had ever laid eyes on. All I could do was stare as her beauty had me momentarily mesmerized.

"Hi, you must be Jordan. I'm Mia," she said in a sexy voice.

"Nice to meet you," I said, but I wasn't just saying it, I meant it. Damn! She was fine and she knew it too.

While everyone stood around talking, Mia walked over to Pedro and kissed him on the cheek.

"She's fine, huh? That's Pedro's fiancé," Chico said.

"Yeah, she's okay," I said, taking a seat on the sofa.

"Do you like any of the girls?" Chico whispered, taking a seat next to me.

"Yeah, they're all nice."

"Well, whatever one you want is yours."

"What?"

"You heard me. Anyone you want you can have."

If only he knew that the one I wanted was marrying his brother and was off limits. "I like her," I said, pointing at the tall, dark, slim one.

"Who Vanessa? No problem. You can have her tonight."

"I like her too," I said.

"That's Suzy. I knew you would like those big titties," Chico said, smiling.

The sound of the loud doorbell rang. Ruiz walked over and opened the door. A tall, dark-skinned man with a policeman's uniform walked in.

"Tucker, what took you so long?" Chico asked, standing up, giving the man a hug.

"I had to lock up some drug dealers," he said as everyone burst out laughing—everyone except me.

"Tuck, this is my friend I told you about," Chico said.

"Jordan, right?"

"Yeah, what's up?" I said, standing up shaking his huge hand.

"I heard you're one helluva basketball player."

"I can hold my own."

"We're gonna have to play a one-on-one some day. I'm tired of whipping on these bums," he said, pointing at Pedro, Chico and Sid.

"That's fine with me. I would love to."

"Jordan is the man, Tuck. He will bust your ass," Chico said.

"That's what you said about Sid, and I beat him four games straight."

"I didn't feel like playing that day," Sid hollered across the room.

Tucker was a dark-skinned, tall man about six-three with extra large hands. He looked like a baller, but it really didn't matter. Personally, I don't think anybody on the planet could stop me one-on-one.

"Tucker is a cop from the LAPD. Our number one man," Chico said, putting his arm around him.

"I've got to get back to work before the captain starts wondering where I am," he said.

"It's upstairs, Tuck, in the back room. I'll call you later," Chico said.

Tucker quickly ran upstairs.

"Come on everybody, let's go out by the court," Pedro said.

Everyone followed Pedro out to the court. Turning around, I noticed Tucker walking out the door holding two large green army duffle bags.

As we all walked out back, Chico and I took a seat on the bench and watched the four lovely women play a game of two-on-two basketball. Pedro and Mia sat by the pool hugging and kissing like lovers do while Sid sat on a beach chair by the pool talking on his cell phone.

"What's up, Chico? What did you want to tell me that's so important," I said.

"I need you," he said, looking me straight in my eyes.

"Need me for what? What do you mean?"

"I need you to be down with us. I want you to be a part of this."

"A part of what? Chico, I don't know what the hell you do."

"You know what we do, don't be stupid, Jordan."

"Why me? Why me, Chico?"

"Because you're one of only two people in the world I totally trust."

"Who else do you trust?"

"My brother Pedro."

I said nothing as a smile appeared on my face.

"Remember when we were in prison and I told you that one day I would give you half of whatever I earned."

"Yeah, I remember when you said it."

"I meant it, every word. I want you to become our partner. Me, you and Pedro."

"What?"

"We will show you everything. He thinks bringing you into the family is a good idea also."

"Why me?"

"Because you're from Philadelphia."

"So what. What does that have to do with anything?"

"It's got to do with everything. Philly is on the east coast. We will be able to expand our business. We will supply you with whatever you want and you'll be able to supply Philadelphia."

"There's plenty of cocaine in Philly," I said. "Yeah, but not for $10,000 a kilo," Chico smiled.

"Ten thousand a key! Damn!"

"Yeah, we will give you 500 kilos at a time. That's five million dollars. Half of that is yours."

"What! Two million, five hundred thousand!"

"All yours. We will get you set up in Philly and send Sid out there with you to get things off the ground. I will front you $250,000 to move your family into a nice house away from the city. You can pay me back once you're done."

"Before I answer you, can you tell me what's really going on," I said.

"This is all I can tell you, Jordan. We have a connect out of Mexico that brings us 2000 kilos at a time. Tucker has friends who work at the border who help us get them through. With your help, we can have both coasts locked down, east and west. But only with your help," Chico said.

"I'll do it," I said, shaking my head. "Yeah, I'll do it."

"The money is in your trunk."

"What?"

"Yeah, the $250,000 is in the trunk of your Mercedes. I *knew* you would say yeah," Chico smiled. "I *knew* you would."

Watching us the whole time, Pedro put up his thumb. I guess that was his way of saying welcome to the family. After everyone had gone back inside the house, I opened up the trunk of my new car. Inside the trunk was a black briefcase. The stacks of brand new hundred dollar bills stared at me in my surprised face. I then close both the briefcase and trunk of the car and walked back inside with the others. Never realizing that I was being watched by Chico the entire time.

"Are you a believer *now*?" Chico asked me, waiting for answer.

All I could do was smile and shake my head.

Later that night, Vanessa and Suzy were both in my room. "What is it that you like, Jordan?" Vanessa said, as she took off her clothes.

"I like *everything*," I said, lying back on the king-size bed. Suzy then walked from out of the bathroom totally nude. Lying on the bed next to me, I began to suck on her big juicy titties. Vanessa then joined the two of us and started sucking my hard dick. As I continue to enjoy Suzy's perfect breast I never heard the knock at the door. I was too busy enjoying this wonderful party of three to put any of my attention elsewhere. Suddenly the door swung open.

"Hi, its us, can we join y'all?" a sweet voice said.

"Come on, girls," Suzy yelled out, "what took y'all so long?"

Opening the door. Christion and Kondi both walked in with long white robes on.

"We were in the Jacuzzi," Christion said.

"Whoa!" I said, "This must be heaven."

"We won't hurt you," Cristina said, smiling, as she and Kondi started taking off their clothes.

"Chico said he wanted you to enjoy yourself. So just relax. We'll take care of you *all* night," Kondi said.

"*All night*! Whoa!"

"All night, *big boy*," Cristina said. "*All* night long."

All night I made love to these four beautiful women, experiencing positions I never knew existed.

After six years of being in prison, they definitely got what they were looking for, one big black backed up nigga. So me being up all night was no problem at all. I fucked them so good and hard that before the sun came up, they were all knocked out on the bed. And I still wanted some more.

As I lay back on the bed that night, I thought about everything that had happened that day, the car, the money, the women, and Chico. Then I thought about my mother and Marquise and a smile came to my face. At last, my mother would get out of that small two-bedroom apartment and quit her two jobs. I couldn't believe this was all happening. I still thought I was dreaming until Vanessa woke up and grabbed my dick and began sucking it again with her soft juicy lips. Then I knew this was no dream. Everything was real.

Chapter 9

A few days later...

Chico and Pedro had everything ready. The owned a large tractor trailer that brought my car back to Philly. Inside the trailer were six large commercial arcade games with 125 kilos packed neatly inside of them. The other two games were both empty and first in line for security purposes. Pedro and Chico owned a company called P&C Video Arcade Game Distributors as a front for the operation. No one suspected that the brothers were actually distributing kilos of cocaine to many sources around the country.

Besides being one of the major cocaine suppliers in south central and southwest L.A., the brothers had other operations in Chicago and Washington, D.C.

I had learned that Officer Sam Tucker had been on their payroll for two years and would sell kilos from his own police cruiser. He had been on the LAPD for eight years and now he was a member of the L.A. drug task force, the same unit that confiscated the drugs off the streets. He also had a big gambling problem where he would bet thousands of dollars on one-on-one basketball games. I also found out that Chico and

Pedro had different fathers. When his family moved to east L.A. from Mexico, Chico's mother had an affair with a black man. Once Chico was born, her husband left his family and never returned. Now I understood why Chico was a little darker than Pedro and much bigger. Chico had never known his own father who also had disappeared. The closest the boys ever had to a father was Ruiz who had known both of them since they were two little kids running up and down the congested streets of east L.A.

In 1989, Chico and Pedro's mother died from complications of AIDS. She was only thirty-two years old when she surrendered her life to the deadly disease. Ruiz told me that the portrait on the wall was of her and that every year on June nineteenth, her birthday, they would have a large celebration in memory of Maria Chicarro, their mother.

After spending four wonderful and memorable days in L.A. I was to catch my plane back to Philadelphia with Sid. While I was here, Chico took me on a tour of the Los Angeles neighborhood. We went from shopping in Beverly Hills to sitting front row at an L.A. Clippers game. From the Redondo Beach to Pasadena, Wilshire Boulevard to Ventura Boulevard. L.A. was the shit!

We even visited friends of his in Watts, and east L.A. where the gang life was more real than I had ever imagined. I realized at that moment that only three things truly mattered on the deadly streets of Los Angeles—Red, Blue and Green.

Sid was Pedro's right hand man and now he would be working with me in Philly. Short and stocky, Sid could pass for a twin brother of Mike Tyson. He was from Eighty-seventh Street in south central L.A. A former gang banger, he lived by the code of the streets and took no shit. Just the type of guy I needed around me, because I had big plans and one thing for sure—every general needs soldiers. There was definitely a war going on on the streets. A war I planned on winning. The bad part about the war we young hustlers face everyday on these mean streets is that no one ever wins. Some people make it others can't take it. But nobody ever really wins. Prison or death is always the outcome, but it's a chance we all take. For some reason, every hustler in the game believes he will be the one who makes it, the one who succeeded, where so many had failed.

Personally, I believe it's ·the challenge—us against the world. What is life without a challenge? Once I was told that every natural life form on earth has an enemy. For every hustler, pimp, gangster, baller, and player—the streets are *ours*.

April 8, 1998, six weeks later...

The first thing I did was buy my mother a beautiful split level six-bedroom home with a two car garage. The house was located in Bryn Mawr, Pa., a suburb of Philadelphia. She was extremely surprised when she walked into the garage and saw the all white 1998 Cadillac STS Seville parked with a red bow around it with the words, "Thanks Mom." written on the front windshield. I had took Marquise and Shawn both shopping at the mall, buying them both brand new wardrobes full of all the latest name brand items.

Uncle Paul decided to get down with us too and supplied us with plenty of new guns. From being a bodyguard for so many people, most of my clientele came from him and his many connections with people in the industry and on the streets. I got myself a luxury apartment in center city that had a beautiful view of downtown. Now every weekend, Marquise would come stay with me.

Business was good. After selling the 500 kilos and paying back the $250,000 that Chico lent me, every two weeks another 500 kilos of cocaine was sent, packed neatly inside of video arcade games.

After I opened up and took the drugs from inside the arcade games, I would neatly stack the money inside and close it back up, sending the arcade game and the money back to California. Once things got off the ground, Sid went back to L.A., but every two weeks, Chico and Sid would fly to Philly to hangout with me and discuss business. No one knew anything about me, which made everything perfect. My mother would always say, Everyone who chooses to shine would be the one who get the time. And everyone who stays low key and clever, will last forever. Mom was always right.

Life was good now. Everything was finally coming together. Now all I had to do was find Cookie and help her put her troubled life together.

Santa Monica, California… Monday night.

"What do you mean the shipment was confiscated?" Pedro said, pacing around the living room. Sid and Chico were both sitting on the sofa.

"My friends at the border needed a bust. Too much has been getting through without anyone getting arrested. It was time."

"That was 3000 kilos, Tucker. Why couldn't they get a smaller bust?"

"What do we pay them for?" Chico said.

"Don't worry, don't worry, the next shipment will get through."

"Fuck that! My connect will be very disappointed with

this news," Pedro said. "That's 3000 kilos at $2500 a piece. That's seven million, five hundred thousand he's losing, almost eight million. He will definitely start charging me more. Tucker, you better get your friends at the border straight or I will find somebody else to handle it."

"I'm sorry, Pedro. I'll have a talk with them and straighten things out. Everything would be alright."

"Three thousand kilos! Damn!" Pedro said, banging on the wall.

"You will not have this problem next time, Pedro. I promise," Tucker said.

"I lost millions of dollars with that shipment. Let that be the last time. I'll talk to you later. Please leave now, Tucker."

"I'm sorry, Pedro," Tucker said walking out the door with his head down.

"Where's Mia?" Pedro asked Chico.

"She said she was going over to her mother's house."

"Let everyone know that this week's shipment will be late."

"Okay, I'll call Chicago, D.C. and Philly tonight," Chico said, walking over to his brother.

"Everything will be okay, Pedro. We've lost shipments before."

"Yeah, but never 3000 kilos at one time. I'm going to the boat now. I'll see you later, Chico," Pedro said, walking out of the room.

The boat was a fifty-three foot yacht that Pedro owned. It was docked by a pier off the Pacific Ocean. It's where Pedro would sometimes go to collect his thoughts.

Chico called his connects in Chicago and in D.C.; after telling them that things would be late, he called me.

"Hello," I said, answering my cell phone while driving

down Twenty-first Street in north Philly.

"What's up, Jordan?"

"Chico, what's the deal?" I said.

"I can't come to Philly tomorrow."

"Why not?"

"The arcade games won't be ready till later."

"What happened?"

"We ordered some new pieces for our games and they got stolen."

"Oh, yeah?"

"Yeah, but it will be okay, the arcade games will get there."

"Well, I'm cool right now. I still have a few good machines left."

"I'll talk to you tomorrow. I just wanted to let you know what was going on in California, that's all."

"Cheer up, Chico. You sound like you just lost your best friend."

"I *did*, three thousand of them."

"What!"

"You heard me. I'll call you tomorrow."

"Bye, Chico," I said.

From the sound of Chico's voice, I knew something was wrong. There was something he wanted to tell me, but he couldn't tell me on the phone. I knew Chico. I would always know when something bothered him.

Inside a well-furnished hotel in Beverly Hills...

"He went for it," Tucker said smiling.

"You don't think he suspects anything, do you?" Mia said, laying naked on top of the king size waterbed.

"No, I told him that the border patrol needed the bust."

"What about you?" Tucker said, as he started kissing Mia's back.

"I told Chico to tell him I had to go over to my mom's."

"After a while, you're going to have to use another excuse," Tucker said.

"He doesn't think I'm doing anything. He trusts me," Mia smiled.

"Yeah, he's a sucker for love," Tucker said.

"I can't help it if I'm irresistible. How much did we get for the 3000 kilos?" Mia asked, turning around on her back, showing her perfectly formed body.

"Nine million. I sold them for $3000 a piece."

"When are you going to kill him and get it over with?"

"Soon. Once he let's me know about the next shipment that comes through. I'll let you know what you have to do."

"What about Chico. I don't think he trusts me. He thinks I'm just a gold digger. He never liked me."

"Once Pedro is dead, Chico will need comfort from his friends. He will only trust us and once he does, we'll kill him too."

"Chico is smarter than Pedro. We've got to watch him."

"Fuck Chico! You just make sure you continue playing your part, the loyal, always loving girlfriend. Everything will be okay. After the next shipment, Pedro will be dead and we'll be 9 million dollars richer. Then Chico will be next. Then we can go get married like I promised you and move to Brazil."

"Okay, baby, I'll play lovie dovie a little bit longer."

"It will be all over in a few more weeks, beautiful. Right now, everything is going according to plan. It only took us a year to put things together, a few more weeks and it's all over. Just a few more weeks."

"What about Jordan?"

"Who? Who the fuck is Jordan?"

"Jordan, the guy from Philadelphia."

"If he gets in our way, we'll kill him too. Answer something for me, Mia, there's something I want to know?"

"What? What is it?"

"Did you ever love Pedro?"

"I thought I did at one time."

"Did you ever love anyone else before?"

"Yes. I was in love with someone very deeply."

"Who?"

"It's a long story. He didn't love me. It's over now."

"You sound like you still love him."

"No, it's over."

"When did your love for this man finally end?"

"When Pedro introduced us! When you walked around his swimming pool in those sexy black Speedos, showing your fine tall dark body. I knew I had to have you. I knew one day that I would fuck you. And when you followed my Lexus that time and pulled me over, I swear, my pussy was so wet I could've drowned. That blue uniform turned me on."

"Oh, yeah?" Tucker said smiling. "Yeah, you know it."

"I love you Sam and I want to be your wife. There's nothing I wouldn't do for you."

"I love you too, Mia and everything will turn out fine."

"Now come over here and fuck me with that big, black long, dick of yours. I got to get home to Pedro soon before he starts looking for me."

"Whatever you want," Tucker said as he bent Mia over and began fucking her from behind. "Whatever you want."

Chapter 10

The next day, 2 p.m. in the afternoon…

As I was driving down Eighteenth Street, I spotted Cookie and another woman walking. I pulled over and rolled down my window.

"Cookie, Cookie, come here!" I yelled.

"Jordan, is that you?" she said, staring at my brand new Mercedes.

"Yeah, get in," I said, unlocking the passenger door.

"Hold up one minute, Barb," Cookie said, getting inside the car.

"Jordan, I've been looking for you."

"Yeah, *right*, stop bullshitting me."

"No, I'm serious. I called your mother's house and the phone was disconnected. And I went by there too. Your neighbors said y'all had moved."

"Oh, so you're finally telling the truth about something. What's wrong?" I asked.

"I'm through, Jordan. I'm leaving these streets alone. I miss Marquise so much.

"I'm tired of all this shit, the cops, the tricks, and most of

all Steve. I can't keep living my life like this. Satisfying everyone's needs but my own. Everyday I'm constantly dodging
cops or some crazy ass psycho who preys off women like
myself. There's not a single day that passes that I don't cry or
shed a tear. The last time I felt any kind of happiness was on
Christmas morning with you and Marquise and your family.
And God knows I'll do whatever it takes to have that wonderful feeling back. And another thing, that...

"What tell me," I asked.

"That poem you wrote me just won't leave my mind. It
was beautiful. Please, can you help me get my life together?"
Cookie said, as tears begin falling down her face.

"That's why I was looking for you, to find you and get you
straight. I told you that I would help you. Now I can. I'm on
my way to the airport. I'm going to California. Here's my
mother's new phone number and address."

"I'll be there tomorrow morning," she said.

"Cookie, you better *be* there. I'll be back in two days."

"I will. I promise you."

Looking into Cookie's watery green eyes, I could tell she
was telling the truth as we both smiled and gave each other
hugs.

"Marquise misses you. He always asks about you."

"I miss him too. I can't wait to see him tomorrow."

"Thank you, Jordan. Thank you for everything. You
know I love you, right?"

"I know, Cookie. I love you too."

"Tomorrow morning, I'll be there, I promise."

"Do you need any money?"

"No, I'm fine. I have enough for a cab to get me to your
mother's house."

"Where are you going now?" I asked, as Cookie was getting out of the car.

"Over to Barbara's house, I have clothes and Marquise's baby pictures over there. And I want to say goodbye to the girls."

"Okay, I'll see you in a few days."

"Yeah, then you can tell me about this brand new Mercedes you're driving around," Cookie said, smiling.

"Goodbye, Cookie. Tomorrow morning, don't forget."

"I won't," Cookie said, waving, as I pulled off and cruised down the street leaving her and the other woman's eyes following me as I drove away.

Picking up my cell phone, I called my uncle Paul.

"Hello," he said, answering the telephone.

"Unc, what's up? It's me."

"Jordan, where are you?"

"I'm on my way to the airport."

"Is everything okay?"

"Yeah. I'm just going to see Chico. I'll be back in a few days. I need you to handle things while I'm away."

"I'll take care of everything. Don't worry."

"Okay, Unc, see you in a few days," I said.

Turning up my car's stereo, I enjoyed the smooth soulful sounds of WDAS FM, as I headed toward Philadelphia International Airport.

Santa Monica, California...

Pedro and Chico were both sitting in the living room just after Mia had left to go over to her mother's home.

"You love that girl, don't you?" Chico said.

"I love her to death. That's why I'm marrying her. Chico,

please don't start. I do not want to hear any of your lectures today."

"I'm just looking out, that's all. Once you get married, you know she's entitled to half."

"So? She'll be my wife."

"At least think about a prenup Pedro, she shouldn't have a problem with that."

"I'll think about it, Chico."

"I still think she's a phony. A fucking gold digger."

"Chico, can you please don't say anything about her, if you don't have anything good to say out of your mouth."

"All she does is shop! And spend money. I still think she's using you, Pedro. You bought her mother a house, her older sister a house and her a Lexus."

"What's wrong with that?"

"Nothing, if it's out of love."

"I do love her."

"But, does she *love* you?"

"Yes, she tells me all the time. I'm all she thinks about. She constantly reminds me of how I'm the only man she's ever made love to."

"I think you should have left her broke ass in Compton."

"Chico, that's it, now stop."

"Alright, but can you just do one favor for me? One favor and I'll never question her again."

"What? What's that?"

"Can you just get someone to follow her for a few weeks. At least before y'all two get married."

"A private eye?"

"Yeah. I mean if she's everything you say, it shouldn't matter."

"I trust her. It would all be worthless."

"Pedro, nothing in this life we live is worthless. Everything and everyone should always be checked out. In this game, it's the people who are closest that take you down. At least, let me make sure that those who claim to be our friends truly are."

"Okay, okay, Chico, go ahead. You can hire a private eye. Only for two weeks. Not a day longer. But you'll see that what I'm saying is right."

"If I'm wrong I'll apologize and never disrespect your fiancé again. Now let me get things ready before Jordan gets here."

"Jordan is coming tonight?"

"Yeah, he's flying in from Philly."

"What's up?"

"Four things."

"What's that?"

"Vanessa, Suzy, Cristina and Kondi," Chico said, as he and Pedro both started laughing.

"Man, that guy is a beast. How does he do it?"

"That's what six years will do to you."

"Ruiz, Ruiz," Chico called out.

"Yes, Chico, what do you need, sir," Ruiz said, walking into the room.

"Can you call the girls? Jordan will be here later."

"Sure. Anything else?"

"No, just tell them to be here by nine, that's all."

"Okay, sir. I'll take care of it as soon as possible," Ruiz said, leaving the room.

"What are you doing tonight, Pedro?"

"Mia and I are going out tonight when she returns from her mother's."

"Okay, I'll see you later," Chico said, walking up the stairs.

Philadelphia

In a small row home on Fifteenth Street in North Philadelphia, Barbara and a few other women were helping Cookie pack her clothes and belongings. As the women were all laughing, Steve and RW walked in. Suddenly, all of their smiles quickly changed.

"What the hell is going on? One of you bitches had better answer or all of you will be dead whores tonight. It looks like someone is trying to leave. Is it your Barbara? Are you running out on me?" Steve yelled.

"No Steve." Barbara said.

"Bitch don't you *lie* to me!" Steve said, grabbing a fist full of her long black hair.

"Let her go Steve! I'm the one leaving, Cookie shouted. I'm going home to my son. I'm through with this shit! After releasing Barbara, Steve quickly reached out and grabbed Cookie by her shirt collar. "Bitch are you stupid or just plain crazy?"

"You don't leave Steve. No bitch leaves Steve," he said.

"Steve, she wants to get her life straight," Barbara yelled. "*Fuck* her life!" Steve said. "Bitch you better shut up or you're next."

"I just want to go take care of my child. Please Steve that's *all* I want." Cookie begged.

"Look whore I own you. I'm your daddy. I feed you, you slut. When that no good of a man of yours got locked up, I took care of you and that little bastard. Bitch, how could you just leave me," Steve said, smacking Cookie to the floor. "Fuck you Steve! I'm tired of you and I'm tired of living like this," Cookie said, fighting back. With his left hand Steve once again smacked Cookie across her face sending her to the floor. Steve kicked her in the stomach. Steve stood over her as she lay on the floor holding her stomach.

"Do you know what happens when you betray me bitch? Do *you*?"

"Fuck you Steve!" Cookie said, with blood falling from her mouth. Putting the gun between her tearful green eyes, Steve asked again, "Do you know, I said bitch, do you hear me talking to you?"

"Please Steve! Please don't..." Barbara yelled.

"You end up dead whore," Steve said, as he pulled the trigger releasing a life-ending bullet to Cookie forehead.

Cookie's body slumped to the ground. Tears from all the girls started to fall as they all looked at their good friend lying dead on the cold floor.

"Any of you bitches ever try and leave me, the same will happen to you. Do I make myself clear?" Steve said, looking at all the frightened women.

All of them agreeably shook their heads fearing for their own life.

"If any of you bitches says anything about this to anybody, I will kill you. Then I will kill you're fuckin' families. All of you, get the fuck out of here and get back to work," Steve yelled.

Each woman quickly stepped over Cookies' dead body and rushed out the door.

"Hold up, Barbara. You stay."

Nervously shaking, Barbara stopped at the door.

"You help RW clean this mess up. I don't want a trace of blood on this floor."

"Everything will be taken care of Steve," RW said, laying Cookie's coat over her face.

"I'll be back. I got to go change my clothes. The whore got blood on my new jeans," Steve said, putting his gun in his pocket. "I'll be back in an hour," he said, walking out the door.

Bryn Mawr, Pa...

That night as my mother was laying on her bed reading her bible, a soft knock at her door interrupted her.

"Who is it?" she asked.

"It's me, Grand mom, Marquise."

"Come in."

Opening her door, Marquise walked in and sat on the bed beside her.

"What's wrong? Why aren't you asleep? You have school tomorrow."

"I can't fall asleep, grand mom. I keep waking up."

"Why can't you go to sleep, Marquise?"

"My mommy," Marquise said.

"Your dad is going to find your mom and help her."

"She's gone."

"He will find her."

"She's gone, Grand mom. My mommy is gone."

"She'll come back and everything will be alright. Come get under the covers. Tonight you can sleep with me."

Getting under the covers, Marquise tightly held her.

"Go to sleep. Everything will be okay," she said, running her hand through his curly hair.

"She's gone," Marquise said, before closing his eyes and falling asleep.

Chapter 11

That night while driving on the freeway coming back from Downtown L.A., Chico and I were inside his red ferrai talking.

"What's wrong, Chico? You've been on cloud nine all night."

"I've got so much *shit* on my mind. That's why I picked you up at the airport to clear up my head."

"You're too young to be stressing. Keep it up and you'll be bald by thirty."

"I just don't understand why Pedro is tripping over that bitch."

"That's his fiancé, it's who he loves."

"I just think something is up with her. Something isn't right. Pedro is so caught up in her beauty, he's getting side tracked."

"What man wouldn't? Mia is one fine chick."

"I wouldn't! I see through that phony act she's putting on."

"Didn't you say that you were getting a private eye to check her out?"

"Yeah, but I lied."

"Oh, you're not now?"

"No. I already had one. I hired a guy named Tom Leavy a few weeks ago. He's going to let me know whatever he can find out at the end of the month. I paid him to watch Mia for a month."

"Well then, you'll have all of your answers soon."

"It's not just that, Jordan, it's everything. Pedro was never like this before he met Mia. He never tripped over a female like this."

"Stop worrying yourself crazy. Pedro can handle himself."

Chico picked up his cell phone and called home.

"Hello," Ruiz said, answering the phone.

"Where's Pedro, Ruiz?"

"He and Mia left in the Porsche about twenty minutes ago."

"Is everything ready?"

"Yes, Chico, all the girls are here. They've been waiting for a while."

"I'll be there shortly."

"Okay, Chico, I'll let the women know."

Chico continued to drive heading towards home.

Staring at the beautiful Pacific Ocean from a high gaited cliff, Pedro and Mia were inside his white Porsche talking. The dark sky was filled with bright stars on this calm night while a half moon looked down at them through the sunroof.

"Is your mother feeling alright?" Pedro asked.

"Yeah, she's getting better. She's been enjoying my company for the last few weeks, and I've been enjoying hers."

"I'm glad she's doing okay. Now we can start spending some quality time together."

"She just needed me there," Mia smiled. "Pedro, baby."

"Yes, Mia," Pedro said, running his hand through her hair.

"Do you think you can do me a small favor?"

"What is it?"

"I want a new car."

"I just bought you the Lexus."

"I don't like it anymore. It stopped on me the other day."

"You only had it for three months. I'll get it checked out."

"I just want something different. Everybody has a Lexus."

"What do you want?"

"A Jag! A convertible Jag," Mia said, in a sweet sexy voice. "Please. Please."

"I'll think about it."

"I'm going to be your wife soon and I want to represent my man to the fullest. The only man I ever loved and the only man I've ever been with."

"What about your new Lexus?"

"I'll give it to my little brother. He needs a car. He'll get it fixed."

Leaning over, Mia unbuttoned Pedro's jeans. Pedro didn't say a word as a smile came to his face.

"Will you just think about it?" Mia asked, as she held his hard dick in her hand.

"I'll think about it. I promise I'll give it some thought."

Mia gently wrapped her soft lips around Pedro's dick. In a slow motion, she maneuvered her head up and down. Pedro's eyes immediately closed as the wonderful sensation ran through his entire body.

Slipping her thong off from under her dress, Mia sat up and climbed on top of him. She reclined the seat and aggressively began riding him as he held on to her hips. Instantly, her wetness covered all of him. Pedro grabbed her long black hair and they began passionately kissing.

"Oh, Oh, Ohh, Mia you feel so good," Pedro said, as he came.

Mia continued to ride him non-stop. "Oh, ohhh," Come again. I want you to come again," she screamed.

Up and down she went until she finally had an orgasm and Pedro's dick could stand no more.

As she remained laying on top of him, she whispered in his ear, "I love you, Pedro."

"I love you too, baby," he said, as his drained body slumped in the chair.

After entering the house, Chico and I went upstairs to my room. Opening the door the sight of four beautiful women all laying on the bed surprised me.

"What took y'all so long?" Christion said, smiling, as me and Chico walked in and shut the door. "It don't matter we're here now," I said.

"We've been waiting for hours," Kondi said, as she and the rest of the girls began slowly undressing. Then they began to undress Chico and me. Christion walked over and turned on the CD player. The smooth mellow love making music instantly flowed throughout the room. "I want it from the back," Venessa said, bending over in front of me, showing off her pink lips and hairy pussy. "Me too," Kondi said, and bending over in front of Chico who was now fully erect and ready to relieve some stress.

As both of these lovely women faced each other, Chico and I began fucking them from behind. Suddenly the two women started kissing each other as the two of us continued to stroke them from the back. While the four of us indulged in our wonderful sexual and explicit act, in the sixty-nine position, Suzy and Christina began eating each other's pussy. For the remainder of the night, the six of us enjoyed this marvelous and private orgy.

That night, Chico and I made love several times to each woman and the four of them made love to one another.

I remember when Chico and I were in prison and the two of us would both fantasize about the sexual acts we would do with women, once we were both released. We would talk about having sex with different races of beautiful women from all around the world, black, white, Asian, Spanish, but never in my wildest and lustful thoughts did I ever think our simple little male conversations would actually one day come true.

When I returned home from my two-day adventure, I received the shock of my life. While reading through the *Philadelphia Daily News,* I ran across a small article about a prostitute found dead in North Philadelphia. It was Cookie's slain body laid slumped inside a trash dumpster that was found behind a Chinese grocery store. The paper said her body had been there for at least twenty-four hours and she had been shot once in the head. The pain that I felt that day is a pain that has never left my soul. The only woman that I had ever truly loved and the mother of my child was dead at twenty-three years old, becoming another victim to these cruel and unforgiving streets.

Everyone had known about Cookie's death except Marquise. My mother and I decided that I should be the one who told him that his mother had died. So that day, I waited for him to come home from school.

Entering his bedroom, the sight of seeing me sitting on his

bed brought a smile to his little face, as he ran to me and gave me a hug.

"Daddy, Daddy. I miss you," he said.

"I miss you too, little man," I said controlling my tears that wanted to fall. "I have to talk to you, buddy."

"Okay," he said, taking off his backpack and sitting next to me on the bed.

"Yes, Daddy, what is it?" he said, looking into my eyes.

For some reason, I believed he knew something had happened to his mother. For some strange reason, I could tell he just knew.

"Yes, Daddy, tell me what's wrong."

Clearing my throat, I could no longer control the tears in my eyes, as I calmly said, "Your mother is gone. Your mother died."

Marquise said nothing as he just gave me a hug. Holding me tightly in his little arms, he looked into my sad eyes and said, "Daddy, please stop crying. I know my mommy is gone."

Shocked and confused, "You know!" I said.

"Yes, I already know."

"How, who told you?"

"God told me daddy. God told me the other night," Marquise said, laying his head on my chest. Looking up I noticed my mother standing in the doorway crying the whole time.

I just sat there speechless, yet confused at the same time. Here I was with a flow of tears falling from my eyes and Marquise never shed a tear once. My seven-year-old child comforted his saddened father. A child who had just lost his mother, still he showed no emotions or fear.

For the next couple of days, Uncle Paul and I searched the

whole entire North Philly for answers. With a loaded 9-mm on my hip and another one inside my glove compartment, someone was going to pay for killing my son's mother. I was determined to find out who killed her and left Cookie's body inside a trash dumpster. But no one knew anything. Nothing!

I knew from talking to Cookie that last time that she was serious about changing her troubled life around and becoming a mother to our child once again, but something happened that ended her life. Something went wrong that day. Something that no one would tell us as we continued to look for answers, but I was determined to find out.

Chapter 12

A week after Cookie's funeral, I picked up Marquise from school. Uncle Paul was taking care of the street business which gave me more time to spend with Marquise. Driving on the expressway, I had my eyes on the road when Marquise opened the glove compartment.

"Daddy, is this yours?" he said, pointing to the 9-mm that was inside.

"Shut that! You stay away from them. Guns are bad," I said, reaching over and closing the glove compartment.

"I'm sorry, Dad," he said.

"Guns hurt people, Marquise," I said pulling off the expressway.

Later that night, after tucking Marquise into bed, I was sitting in the living room watching TV when the phone rang.

"Hello," I said, picking up the phone.

"Yes, can I speak to Jordan?" a beautiful voice said.

"This is Jordan speaking. Who is this?"

"This is Barbara."

"Barbara?"

"I'm a friend of Cookie's."

"Oh shit! I didn't know your name; I've been looking for you and couldn't find you anywhere. You or any of the other girls."

"We moved to another location."

"So what's up Barbara?"

"I know what happened to Cookie," she said

"You know?"

"Yes, I know everything. Everything that happened."

"Who?"

"I can't say it on the phone, but if you can meet me, I will tell you everything."

"Where are you?" I asked.

"I'm in North Philly, but we can't meet here. Too many eyes and ears."

"Where can I meet you? I'll come get you."

"You can meet me in front of the movie theater on Twelfth and Chestnut. I'll be there in an hour."

"Okay, fine. I'll be in a black Mercedes Benz."

"I'll see you in an hour," she said, hanging up the phone.

After hanging up the phone, I called Uncle Paul. I then picked him up at his apartment and we both went to meet this woman named Barbara.

Outside the Twelfth Street movie theater, I pulled into an empty car space. Holding a loaded .45 in his hand, my Uncle Paul remained calm. Uncle Paul didn't trust anybody, man or woman, everybody was a threat, he would say.

As we sat waiting, Barbara appeared as she walked from around the corner. In a long black mink coat and six-inch heels, she walked towards my parked car. Though I had seen her before, I didn't realize to this day how beautiful she was.

But she was fine. Looking at her dark brown complexion with a sexy dark mole on her left eye, made me wonder why this attractive black woman was out selling herself for peanuts and not collecting millions on somebody's runway.

"Sit in the front," Uncle Paul said, opening the door and getting in the back seat.

Taking a seat, she shut the car door. "Can we go somewhere?" she said.

"Where?" I asked, staring in her beautiful brown eyes.

"Just drive," she said looking all around out the window.

Pulling out of my space, I drove down Chestnut Street.

"Hi, I'm Barbara," she said, shaking my hand and then Uncle Paul's.

"So what do you know, Barbara?" I asked.

"I know who killed Cookie."

"Who?"

"His name is Steve."

"Steve!" I said, shocked.

"Yes, me and six other girls work for him. He drives a green Lexus…"

"I know what he drives," I said in an angry voice.

"You know him?"

"No, not really, but I know of him."

"What happened?" I said, as I continued to drive.

"She wanted to leave. She was through and wanted to go back to her son."

"Then what?"

"Steve came by my apartment and found out she was trying to leave. He was very upset and slapped her. He asked her how could she do this to him after all he had done for her. He said *you* had run out on her and he was the one who took care of her and Marquise. She cried, but he didn't care. That's when he pulled out the gun... and shot her in the head. Then he told us that if anyone said a word, he would kill us *and* our families. Then he told everyone to go except his bodyguard RW and me. He said we had to clean up the place.

"I went through Cookie's pockets and found a piece of paper with that number on it, and this."

She Pulled out a small picture and passed it to me. It was a photo of Cookie and me when she visited me in prison, holding our newborn baby, Marquise, in her arms.

"She would always talk about you. She loved you. I remember Steve trying and trying so hard to take her out. She would always turn him down. After a while, she finally agreed. And slowly he became her downfall. Cookie was beautiful and Steve used her, introducing her to drugs then eventually prostitution. The same thing he does to all his women. Steve preys off beautiful, vulnerable women whose men are either in jail or dead. This is how he gets us, with lies and false illusions."

"What about *you*?" I asked.

"I never did drugs. I was one of the only few girls who didn't. Steve isn't my predator. He is my protection. I just needed someone to look after me on these streets. So I paid him a percentage of what I made just for his protection. Eventually, he put me in charge of all the girls. That's how Cookie and I became friends. I thought she was so beautiful with her green eyes and long black hair. Many times I tried to convince her to leave, but the drugs were stronger than I had thought. Cookie and I had so much in common. Both our men were gone. My husband was murdered in '93 and we both had little boys. She would bring Marquise over to play with Sharrod, my son, all the time. He's nine years old and now lives with my sister in

South Philly."

"Do you know where Steve lives?" Uncle Paul asked.

"No. I only have his cell phone and pager number. He comes and goes. But he and his bodyguards do keep a close eye on us; he's over-protective when it comes to his girls. And most of our clientele know Steve and know that what would happen if they tried something stupid. The girls all have shifts and I collect the money."

Pulling over on a small quiet street, I parked my car. "Would you help me? I asked.

"Yes, Steve deserves whatever he gets for killing Cookie. What do you want me to do?"

"I need you to just call him and meet him. We'll handle the rest."

"I'll do it. He's out of town for a few days. RW is in charge of everything."

"Can you call RW?" Uncle Paul said from the back seat.

"Yes, I have his cell phone number too."

"What about tomorrow?" I asked.

"Tomorrow's fine. Friday is our biggest day. He'll let me know where to meet him when I call."

"Where will you be working tomorrow?" I asked.

"On the corner of Broad and Master. The girls and I will be there all night. RW drives a silver Pathfinder. He's usually driving around the neighborhood looking out for cops and watching out for us."

After the three of us planned everything out, I dropped Barbara back on Twelfth and Chestnut Street. Watching her turn the corner, she disappeared.

I decided that Barbara would call him first and meet him so Uncle Paul and I could see who this person was. Then a few hours later, she would call him again. And that's when we would get him.

Barbara also told us that all the girls were fed up with Steve and were willing to work for someone else if Steve was killed.

Before I dropped Barbara off, we had exchanged numbers. She would be looking forward to my call Saturday afternoon.

Beverly Hills Hotel, Hollywood, California...

Mia and Tucker had just finished making love and now were laying on the bed talking.

"A few more days and it will be all over, baby," Tucker said, as he was kissing around Mia's soft round ass.

"The shipment will be here by Tuesday, Pedro told me yesterday at the house. Once it's safe and away, we'll be ready for plan B and he'll definitely bite. Once he shows up, he'll never know what hit him," Tucker said smiling. "Are you ready?"

"I've been ready for a year," Mia said, enjoying the warm tongue that was slivering around her ass. "He'll show up as soon as I call him, like he always does."

"Did you tell him about the car?"

"Yeah, I told him that it had been stopping on me sometimes."

"Did he believe you?"

"He believes everything I tell him."

"Then everything is set. Tuesday night, he'll be dead and we'll eventually be 3000 kilos richer."

"Then Chico will be next, just like we planned, right?" Mia said.

"That's right, beautiful, Chico will be next."

Tucker rolled Mia over onto her back and began kissing

her around her plumped round breast. Lifting both her long slim legs onto his muscular broad shoulders, he then entered himself into her wet pussy.

Her hard moans instantly began as he deeply stroked every bit of his nine-inch dick inside of her. Though Pedro paid the bills and bought her cars, jewels and clothes, it was Tucker who satisfied her sexually, and once you controlled the pussy, you controlled the mind.

Chapter 13

Philadelphia's International Airport...

"Why didn't you tell me you were coming today? I would have had some girls ready." I said, as Chico got inside my car.

"I just decided to come on the spur of the moment. I just wanted to get away for a few days."

"Today is a bad day," I said, as I drove out of the airport and down Eighty-fourth Street.

"Why, what's up?"

"My Uncle and I had some important business to take care of."

"What?"

"It's about my son's mother. She's been killed."

"What? Maybe I can help."

"No we can handle it. Its something that I got to do alone."

"Jordan just like in prison we are in this together. You're my best friend and I won't let you go through this without me."

"We found out what happened to Cookie and who's responsible."

"What! Someone knows something? What did you all find out?"

"I found out who killed her."

"Who?"

"A guy named Steve. And he had his bodyguard, some dude named RW, throw her body into a dumpster. Since Steve is out of town, tonight we're going to get the bodyguard. Then when he gets back to Philly, he's next."

"I'll do it for you and fly back to California tonight."

"Thanks, but no. I want to kill them both. Besides, everything is already set. We have everything ready to go."

"At least let me go. You know I'll have your back."

"Okay, you can go for the ride, Chico, but that's it."

"I won't say a word," Chico said, as I continued to drive home.

Hearing his cell phone ring, Chico answered it. "Hello, who's this?" Chico asked, wondering who was calling him way across the country.

"It's me, Tom Leavy," a voice said.

"Oh, Tom, what's up?"

"I have what you requested."

"When can I get it?" Chico smiled.

"Monday evening, you can come pick it up at my office in L.A."

"Well, I won't be back to the city till Tuesday night."

"When you're ready, they'll be here."

"Can you take them to my house?"

"Sure, if that's what you want."

"I'll tell my butler, Ruiz, you're coming by. You can give it to him."

"Okay. That's fine. I'll drop all of your material off on

Monday at the house."

"Thanks, Tom."

"Thank you, Chico. I hope you enjoy what I have for you."

"For Pedro's sake, I hope I don't," Chico said, in a sad voice.

"I'll call you to let you know I received them next week, Tom."

"Okay, you take care," he said, hanging up the phone. Closing his cell phone, Chico sat back in his seat.

I pulled into the parking lot of my apartment building; Uncle Paul was already waiting inside his large dark blue Ford Expedition with tinted windows.

The three of us then went inside my apartment and waited. I called Barbara on her cell phone; everything was all set to go. Now the four of us would all wait on something that we had no control over … the night to arrive.

Ruiz, do you know where Chico went? He's not in his room," Pedro asked.

"He told me to tell you he was going to Philly to see Jordan."

"Why didn't he tell me?"

"You were asleep."

"Did you see Mia?"

"She ran over to her mother's house. Someone had paged her and said it was an emergency."

"Why didn't she say anything this morning? I would have taken her."

"Maybe she didn't want to wake you."

Pedro picked up the telephone and called Mia's mother's

house.

"Hello," a woman's voice answered.

"How are you, Miss Jones?"

"Hi, Pedro. How are you?"

"I should be asking you. I heard you haven't been feeling too good in the last few weeks."

"I'm feeling better now."

"Is Mia there? I tried her cell phone but she never answered."

"Oh, she left it on the table. She went to the supermarket to pick up a few things."

"When she comes back, tell her to call home please."

"I will, Pedro, soon as she comes back."

"You take care, Miss Jones."

"Thank you, Pedro," she said.

Pedro immediately called Tucker on his cell phone. An answering service picked up. "*Hello, this is Tuck. I'm busy right now taking care of some important business, but if you please leave your name and number, I'll call you back as soon as possible. Thank you.*"

After the beep, Pedro left a message.

"Tuck, it's me, Pedro. Call me back as soon as you finish taking care of your business. I wanted to talk to you and Sid tonight. It's very important."

Pedro hung up the phone and went into his bedroom and shut the door.

Later that night … on a small deserted street a few blocks away from Broad and Master, Chico, Uncle Paul, Barbara and I all sat inside of my uncle's truck.

"Are you ready to call RW," I asked Barbara.

"I'm ready," she said confidently.

"Here," I said, passing her $500.

Every $500 the girls made RW would come pick up. It wasn't safe for any of the girls to walk around with money on them. The females were always an easy target for petty thieves.

Opening her cell phone, she called RW.

"Hello," a hard voice answered.

"It's me, Barbara. I'm ready," she said.

"Damn! That was quick. It's only been an hour."

"It's Friday. Business is good," Barbara said.

"Meet me at the WaWa on the corner of Twelfth Street."

"I'll be there in fifteen minutes," Barbara said, quickly hanging up.

He wants me to meet him at the WaWa on Twelfth Street."

"Okay, we'll go there now. We'll see you when you get there," I said.

Barbara got out of the truck and into her Dodge Caravan that was parked right behind us; the vehicle she would use to pickup and drop off all the girls in.

The three of us then drove to the WaWa. After waiting five minutes, Barbara drove off.

Uncle Paul parked his Expedition after entering the parking lot of the WaWa's. We all noticed that no one was inside RW's pathfinder. A few moments later, RW walked out and sat inside his Pathfinder. Leaving the three of us all momentarily shocked, unable to believe our eyes.

"Oh, shit, do you believe this!" I said, looking at Chico.

"Not if I didn't see it with my own eyes," Chico said.

"Damn!" was all Uncle Paul could say, staring at RW who was eating a hotdog and holding a Coke in his other hand.

"Rodney Walters! That's what RW stands for," I said,

looking at him.

"Yeah, It's his black ass Mother fuckin' Rock! Rodney "Rock" Walters!" Chico said.

Barbara drove up in her Dodge Caravan, parked and got into Rock's Pathfinder.

"You look tense *big* boy." Barbara said, passing RW the money.

"I'm a little tired, I've been up all night."

"Maybe I can help you ease some of that tension," Barbara said, reaching over and rubbing on RW stiff neck.

"Damn that feels *so* good," RW said, closing his eyes.

"It can get much better than this if you let me show you," Barbara said.

"What's gotten into you tonight? Sometime I just look at you and think you're so damn fine RW."

"You do?"

"Yeah, I'm sure the girls told you how much I like you."

"Nope they never told me anything. How much *do* you like me?" RW asked.

"Why tell you when I could *show* you," Barbara said, rubbing on RW's now hard dick.

"You know Steve don't like me to mess with his girls. I supposed to watch out for y'all girls and that's all."

"What Steve don't know won't hurt—will it?" Barbara said, as she continued to rub on RW's dick.

"I guess not, come on let's take a ride for a while."

"No, the girls will know something is up and might tell Steve."

"Then what do you have in mind," RW said.

"How about the next time I meet you we meet on a dark quiet street, there are a few around here.

"That's fine with me, I'll find one for that, you'll never forget," Barbara said, getting out of the Pathfinder.

"Oh I'll be ready," RW said.

After getting back inside of her vehicle, Barbara drove off. Barbara was smooth as they came. Rock then backed out of the parking lot and drove away too.

"What did he say," I asked.

"After some minor convincing he didn't have a problem with it at all," Barbara said.

After everyone left WaWa, Uncle Paul drove back to the small deserted street where Barbara was already waiting. Opening the door, she got back inside the Expedition.

"That was RW," she said, smiling.

But none of us were smiling. Everyone had a serious look on his face.

"What's wrong, y'all look like y'all saw a ghost," she said.

"We did. A ghost from the past," Chico said.

"Y'all know RW from somewhere?" she asked.

"Yeah, we know him very well," Uncle Paul said, hitting his palm with his fist.

"Well, I told him what you said. Next time to meet me on a quiet street."

"What did he say?" I asked.

"He said that he would."

"I have to go check on the girls. I'll see y'all in a few," Barbara said, getting out of the large truck. "I'll be ready," she said, getting back into her van and driving off.

"I still don't believe that RW is Rock," I said.

"Fuck that faggot!" Chico said. "You should let me kill him."

"No, remember, you're staying in the car. Barbara and I

will handle this."

Pulling off, Uncle Paul drove down the dark deserted street.

That evening...

Sitting inside a small furnished room, Pedro, Sid and Tucker were all talking. "Did you talk to your people at the border, Tuck?"

"Yeah, Pedro, everything is set to go. The shipment will get through Tuesday night, everything will be alright," Tucker smiled.

"I don't need any more *fuckups*, Tucker, no more!"

"You won't Pedro. The kilos will be taken to the warehouse and the workers will start putting them into the arcade games for distribution."

"I want you and Sid to be at the warehouse and make sure everything goes right.

"I'll meet Sid there. I'll be a little late."

"Why? What's up?"

"Tuesday, I have a Stop Drugs on our Street meeting at the community center in South Central."

"How long will that take?"

"Not long. When it's over, I'll meet up with Sid at the warehouse."

"Okay, fine. Sid can handle everything until you get there."

The three of them walked out of the room and into the living room where Mia had just walked in.

"Hey, baby," she said, walking up to Pedro giving him a big hug. "My mother told me you called. Is everything okay? I came right over."

"Everything is fine, baby. I just wanted to know where you were."

"I was busy today. Today was a hard day," she smiled, looking at Tucker.

"She told me," Pedro said.

"I am so tired I can hardly move a muscle. I'm going to sleep."

"Stop working yourself so hard."

"I don't mind. It will be worth it, every bit of it," she said, walking up the stairs.

"How's the car holding up?" Pedro yelled.

"It stopped again, but it started back up," Mia yelled back.

"You can drive the Benz. I'll drive the Porsche," Pedro said.

"No, you know what I want to drive," she yelled back down the stairs.

"I'll see you later," Tucker said, walking out the door.

"Me too, Pedro. I'll call you tonight," Sid said, following Tucker out the door.

Sitting down on the couch, Pedro looked up at the large portrait of his mother that was hanging on the wall. "I wish you were here, Mom. I miss you so much. Chico and I miss you so much," he said. Then he kissed his fingers and touched it to their face.

Philadelphia, Pa...

Inside the Ford Expedition, Chico, Uncle Paul and I were waiting for Barbara to show up again. A few moments later she drove up and parked, then got inside Uncle Paul's truck.

"You ready, Barbara?" I asked.

"I'm ready to go," she said.

"Okay, call him now."

Dialing on her cell phone, she called Rock.

"Hello," Rock answered.

"It's me. I'm ready again."

"Damn! Y'all whores are fucking up a storm tonight," Rock laughed.

"Where do you want to meet?" Barbara said.

"There's a small quiet street called Davenport a few blocks down. I'll be waiting inside my Jeep. It's pretty dark too."

"I know where it is. I'll be there in fifteen minutes," Barbara said, hanging up the phone.

"He'll be in his Jeep waiting for me on Davenport Street. It's a small street a few blocks down."

"Is everyone ready?" I asked.

Everyone nodded.

"Can you handle it, Barbara?" I asked.

"No problem, Jordan. My job is simple. You have the hard job."

"Here," Uncle Paul said, passing me a black 9-mm. "Get yourself ready, Jordan, it's time to handle business."

Fifteen minutes later...

Rock was sitting in his Pathfinder waiting for Barbara to arrive. Listening to the radio, he was eating another hotdog that he bought at the WaWa. While Rock was nodding his head to the music, Barbara's Dodge Caravan pulled behind him. Unlocking his passenger's door, Rock continued to nod his head to the music. Opening his door, "Get in," he said, not paying attention. "Oh, shit!" Rock yelled, looking at the front of the 9-mm that was pointed at his chest.

"Barbara, what's going on?" he said, in a terrified voice.

"What the hell is going on?"

Taking off the dark shades and long black wig, Rock looked into my face. With the most terrified look in his startled eyes, "Oh, my God! Jordan!" he said, as I quickly unloaded five piercing bullets into his muscular chest. Still barely alive, Rock opened his driver's door, slumping to the cold ground. Driving up the small dark street, the Ford Expedition pulled beside Rock's bleeding and weakened body. "Help! Help! Help me, please someone help me!" he begged, crawling into the middle of the street.

While Barbara was behind the wheel, and Chico remained sitting in the back seat, Uncle Paul jumped out of the passenger's side, holding his loaded 45.

Chico then rolled down the back window, "Hey, Rock, remember me?"

Rock looked up barely recognizing his face, but the voice was one he had never forgotten.

Uncle Paul then stood over Rock's body and began dumping every single life-ending bullet into Rock's already disabled body. Calmly getting back into the truck, Uncle Paul shut the door.

In Barbara's long black mink coat, I grabbed her wig and shades and quickly got back inside her Dodge Caravan. As the Expedition sped away, I followed it down the street. Into the dark night we all disappeared.

As for Rock, his disfigured and mangled body laid in the middle of the street surrounded by it's own blood, a few feet away from a large trash dumpster. What goes around comes around.

Chapter 14

Bryn Mawr, Pa., Saturday afternoon...

"I have a surprise for you," I said, walking into Marquise's room. Seeing Barbara and Sharrod walk in, he jumped from his bed.

"Sharrod! Aunt Barbara!" he yelled.

"Marquise! We miss you," Barbara said, picking him up, giving him a huge hug. "We miss you so much, Marquise," she cried.

"I miss you too, Aunt Barbara."

"Sharrod, look at all my toys my daddy bought me," Marquise said, pointing to all the toys that were packed neatly in the corner of his room.

"Guess what, Marquise," I said, looking at the smile on his face that I hadn't seen in such a long time.

"What, Daddy?" he smiled.

"Aunt Barbara and Sharrod are going to stay here for a while."

"Ooh, wee," he jumped for joy.

"I talked to Grand mom and she said they could stay as long as they want."

"Thanks, Daddy."

"You're welcome," I said, walking out of his room with Barbara, leaving him and Sharrod alone to play.

"Thank you so much for letting us stay here," Barbara said, wiping the tears from her face. "We really appreciate it."

"I'll do whatever it takes to put a smile on my son's face," I said. "Sharrod can sleep with Marquise in the bunk bed. I'm going out tonight with Chico and Uncle Paul. They're waiting for me at my apartment, but I'll be back later tonight. In the meantime, you can get to know my mom. She's cool as *shit*."

"I'll take care of her," my mother said, walking down the hallway smiling.

"Thank you, Jordan, for everything," Barbara said.

"No. Thank you for everything," I said, walking down the stairs and out the door.

That night, Chico, Uncle Paul and I went out. Eve, a female rap star was having her debut album release party at a popular local club downtown. Uncle Paul had managed to come across some V.I.P. passes from one of his many industry connections. Inside the large club, some of the rap world's most recognized artists roamed about. DMX and the lox stood along the wall with a crowd of infatuated females watching their every move. Jazzy Jeff was even there with a young lady he was promoting named Jill Scott. A few local Philly acts also were there enjoying the new success of Eve. Female rapper, Charlie Baltimore, the Ram Squad, Major Figgaz, and West Philly's underground hardcore rap group Inner City Hustlers filled the large room of fans and celebrities.

"I'm going back over my Mom's house tonight. Y'all can use the apartment if you need it," I said to Chico and Uncle

Paul who were talking to a set of gorgeous, beautiful twins by the crowded bar.

"Yeah, we're gonna need it," Chico said, smiling with one of the beautiful women wrapped in his arms.

After leaving the party, Chico, Uncle Paul and the two lovely twin sisters got inside his Ford Expedition and drove off.

Sleepy and tired, I got into my Mercedes and drove away, headed for my mother's house.

Driving on the expressway on my way over to my mother's house, the thought of Cookie entered my mind. I still couldn't believe she was gone. The only woman I ever loved was now a memory.

I remember when we first met at Sulzberger Junior high school in West Philly. I was the captain and star player of our undefeated basketball team, and she was the high jumping acrobatic captain of the cheerleaders. Everyone thought that we were a match made in heaven. We were even chosen as prom king and queen. And Cookie was picked most likely to succeed. But once she became pregnant at fifteen, things quickly fell apart for both of us. Cookie eventually becoming a young inexperienced mother, and me becoming a former basketball star, with NBA dreams. Now I was a young confused man, stealing cars to support my growing family.

I pulled into the driveway of my mother's house and parked—it was 2:45 a.m. My brother, Shawn, was sound asleep on the living room couch, with the TV still on. I turned it off and walked upstairs to check on Marquise and Sharrod. Opening his door, I saw them knocked out next to each other under the covers. I closed his door and walked down the hall to my mother's room. Right next to my mother's bedroom was the room where Barbara was staying. Tapping once on the door, I heard her voice say, "Come in."

Barbara was sitting on the bed reading the *Philadelphia Daily News.*

"Did you see this?" she said, pointing to an article on page four. *Man found slain on North Philadelphia street*, it said.

"Yeah, I saw it earlier today. I read the whole thing."

"The cops have no clues or witnesses the paper is saying," as Barbara laid the daily news on her night table beside the bed.

"I had a long talk with your mother. You're right, she's cool as shit." Barbara said, changing the subject.

"I told you my mom was cool. Can I have a seat?" I asked.

"Sure, sit down," she said. "She told me that you bought her three bars and one of them she used to work at."

"Yeah, my mom knows how to run them from working in them for so many years."

"She offered me a job."

"She did?"

"She said I could help her manage them."

"What did you say?"

"I said I would love to. Now I can finally put my college degree to some use."

"You went to college?"

"Yeah, I graduated from Drexel University with a degree in accounting."

"How did you end up on the streets?"

"When I got out of college I couldn't find a job. My husband was supporting me and our child all by himself. One day coming from work he was car jacked by two men and shot twice in the head. He died a week later. All my family lives in Virginia. I had nowhere to go so I did what I had to do to support me and my child. A few years later, I met Steve and he became my protection or pimp, whichever one you choose to call him. But I needed some one to watch over me on those streets."

"I told your mother everything today, everything about my whole life. I'm twenty-eight years old. I had promised myself that before I turn thirty, I was going to have my life straight. Your mother said she would help me do it. But I also want to help the other girls; they're lost without me. It's sad, but they need me. Or the same thing will eventually happen to them like what happened to Cookie."

"Well what can you do?" I asked.

"I came up with a good idea for your mother and she liked it."

"What's that?"

"If she could hire the six girls to do bartending, she could teach all of them how to do it since she knows it so well. Two girls could work in each of her bars and I'll make sure all of their money is properly being saved and managed. They are all beautiful women. The men would enjoy seeing fresh pretty young faces, instead of some old grey-haired middle-age man serving them drinks."

"That does sound good," I said, shaking my head in approval.

"Yeah, your mother thought so too."

"I called all the girls. Next week we are going to have a meeting, your mother, all the girls and me. Then they'll start working as soon as possible. This will be our last week working for Steve, and then everyone is leaving him. I figured he wouldn't be around long enough to harass us or threaten our lives."

I said nothing as I sat on the bed admiring her calm demeanor.

"What do you think?" she asked me.

"I think you're a genius," I said smiling.

Rubbing my eyes, Barbara noticed that I was tired. Suddenly she put her warm hands on my shoulders and began massaging my stiff neck and back.

"You're real tense," she said, digging her soothing long fingers into my flesh.

"Yeah, that feels good," I said, closing my eyes, slowly drifting away from the effects of her magical hands.

"Don't fall asleep on me," she said, smiling.

"I'll try not to," I said, sitting back, getting comfortable on the bed.

Lifting my shirt over my head, she threw it on the floor. "If you lay across the bed, I can do a better job," she said.

Lying across the bed, she got on top of me and started massaging my entire back. The feeling was so good as she took her hands up and down my spine in a circular motion.

"Mmmm," I said, enjoying the feeling. "That feels so goood."

"You have a strong back," she said.

But the feeling was too good to respond.

Unbuckling my belt she slowly pulled down my jeans. I didn't say a word, as I let her continue to be in control.

"And the rest of your body isn't bad either," she said, throwing my jeans to the floor next to my shirt.

Slipping off my underwear, she began rubbing around my ass and legs. "I was always told that if you're going to do something, do it right," she said.

Lying on my stomach, I felt her wet warm tongue kissing me down my back. Then it eventually traveled to my ass. My dick instantly got hard as the wonderful sensation ran through my naked body. Taking off her large white T-shirt, Barbara threw it on the floor.

Turning around on my back, I was very much turned on with her beautiful naked body that was in front of me. Her dark brown complexion complimented her perfectly formed figure. I lay there speechless, as I couldn't take my now wide-open eyes off her hairy black pussy.

Standing up, she walked over to the door and locked it. Then she cut off the lights and TV and got back into bed. As I lay on top of the blankets naked, she gently grabbed my hard dick with her warm hands. After rubbing it a few times, I suddenly felt it being swallowed by the wetness of her vibrating tongue. With a slow comfortable motion, she maneuvered her mouth in ways I never experienced before. My body suddenly began shaking as I started coming. Swallowing every bit of what I had released, she then got on top of me. As I sat up on the bed, she put her arms around me and laid her legs on top of my shoulders. "Oh, oh, ohhh, eehhhh, oh, ohhh, ahhhh-hh," she screamed as she slowly rode me in every direction imaginable.

The feeling was so good that I came again, but I was so turned on that my dick just wouldn't go down.

Flipping Barbara over, she wrapped her legs around my waist, as I deeply entered her wet and juicy pussy. At the same time, I was kissing her around her soft neck.

Her light moans became louder, as I aggressively began stroking her with more intense force. "Oh, oh, ohhhh, ummmm," she loudly moaned, as she finally released her orgasm. "Ohhh damn! That felt good," she said, as the sweat from our intense physical workout ran down her beautiful face. "Don't stop! Keep going," she said, putting both her legs behind her head like a trained gymnast. "Ohhh, I'm coming again," she screamed, as I continued to stroke her repeatedly. "Ohhh, God!" she mumbled as her body began shaking uncontrollable. "Ahhhhh," she said, pulling me close to her as we both began kissing passionately. "Ohhh my God!" she yelled out.

No longer could I stand the excitement and this wonderful feeling as I finally came again for the third time.

Tired and sweaty, I slumped to her chest and lay there like a spoiled little child. As we both lay there breathing heavily, I closed my eyes. "That felt *so* good," I said, in a low voice.

"Too damn good!" she said, as I still could feel her body trembling from the after effects of the orgasm.

After kissing me on my forehead, she closed her eyes and the two of us fell asleep in the comfort of each other's arms.

Chapter 15

The next day...

While everyone was still asleep on this early Sunday morning, my mother and I were inside the kitchen talking as she was preparing to fix breakfast.

"Did you enjoy yourself last night," she said, smiling.

"What Mom!" I said, feeling somewhat embarrassed.

"You heard me boy! Did you enjoy yourself," she said, cracking the eggs open putting them inside a large white bowl.

"What are you talking about, Mom?" I said, blushingly.

"All closed eyes aren't asleep," she said, smiling.

"Yeah, I enjoyed myself," I finally said.

"Next time, try and keep it down a little. There are people around here that are trying to sleep."

"I'll buy you some earplugs," I said jokingly.

"I think she's cute," my mother said.

"Yeah, she's pretty," I said.

"Do you know she can cook?"

"No, Mom, I didn't know."

"Well that girl is full of surprises, and very bright, reminds me of myself when I was her age. I like her a lot."

"Mom, guess what," I said, standing up, walking to the door.

"What Jordan?" she said, waiting for an answer.

"Guess, Mom."

"What! Stop playing with me boy."

"I like her a lot too," I said.

A smile then appeared on her face as I walked out of the kitchen.

That afternoon, after everyone had eaten, Barbara and I took Marquise and Sharrod out to see a movie and get something to eat. I told her that I didn't want her to be on the streets any more. But she convinced me that it would be the only way to set up Steve.

"He still had to feel as though he was in control of his girls," she said.

Barbara told me that Steve would be upset about RW's death, but as long as he had his women making money for him, he was okay. He could always hire another gopher—go for this...go for that... like RW.

Tuesday morning, Barbara and the other girls were expecting Steve to be back in Philly. Then he would find out the shocking news of his bodyguard's death.

Uncle Paul and Chico drove to Atlantic City with the twins they met and said they would be back on Monday.

After we had had a fun day out with the kids, I brought them back home and got them ready for bed and school in the morning. While Barbara was tucking the boys in bed, my mother and I were inside her room sitting on her bed talking.

"How was your day?"

"We had fun today, Mom."

"She's a bright girl, isn't she?"

"Yeah, she's got a good head on her shoulders."

"You like her, don't you?"

"I told you I did already."

"No, you really like her."

"What are you talking about, Mom?"

"You don't think I know my own child?"

"She snuck up on you, huh."

"What?"

"You didn't expect this. See how things happened. You never know who or what God has planned for you."

"Yeah, Mom, I like her, but ..."

"But what!"

"But she's a prostitute. Why couldn't she be a doctor or lawyer or something."

"Maybe if she was a doctor or lawyer y'all would never have met, did you ever think of that? Do you know why I left your father, Jordan?"

"No, you never talk about him."

"Do you ever wonder why?"

"All the time," I said, with a confused look on my face.

"Because when you father had no more money and no one or nowhere to turn, you know what he did?"

"What?"

"He abused my love for him and asked me to sell my pussy. Your father became my pimp, the man that I loved more than life itself. I was so stupid and naive that I did it. Because he said it was for us. When all along it was for him. I would sleep with different men and give him all the money. And with the money he would gamble and go spend it on some other bitch. I was a fool for love. One day I just got fed up with everything. While I was lying on my back being fucked by a total stranger and not the man that I love, I laid there crying. I knew that this was the last time I would ever by your father's fool.

"After I was paid, I lied to your father and said the guy didn't give me all of my money. But he did. And I took a few hundred from his wallet while he slept too. Anyway, your father went out to collect the rest of the money he thought the guy owed. When he left and got into his car, I got you dressed and walked out, never to return again, you, me, and $300. I didn't leave a note or anything. I just simply walked away.

"Every time I look at you, I see your father. The difference is that you have my heart. Something he never had. I did the best I could do to raise you by myself. And it was hard being a single parent. But I promised myself and never gave up. So when you look at Barbara, think of your mother, because at one time that was me. And maybe if I had a good man in my corner, maybe I could have become a doctor or lawyer myself.

"What I'm telling you Jordan is, sometime people have no control over their life. Sometimes we get hit with a curve ball. It's not what's on the outside; it's what's on the inside that counts. Don't let your selfish pride ruin a love. In this short life we live in, the only thing that really matters is happiness."

Standing up, I walked to the door and my mother called me.

"Jordan," she said.

"Yes, Mom."

"I see the attraction in both of y'all eyes...don't run away."

I then walked out of her room and shut the door and went downstairs where Barbara was sitting on the couch watching TV.

Sitting down next to her on the couch, I muted the TV

sound with the remote control.

"Hey, I was watching that," she said, in the sweetest voice.

With a serious look on my face, she asked me, "What's wrong?"

"Nothing," I said.

"Something is wrong. What is it?"

"It's about you."

"Me! What about me?"

"Everything."

"Stop speaking in riddles and tell me what you're talking about. Is it what I feel?" she said, looking into my eyes.

"What do you feel?"

"Love and confusion."

"What! That's what you feel?" I said.

"Yup, that's just what I feel. I thought that I could never care for another man after my husband died. But I saw the way you looked at me, and when you asked me to get my son and move to your mother's, my head never stopped spinning. Everyone always thinks about sex first, but you, you're different. You didn't think about that. You thought about my safety and my child, and you didn't even know me. No man would have done what you did. When I first saw you I was attracted to you, when you first drove up looking for Cookie. It was the way you demanded her to come with you, and be there for your child on Christmas morning. I admired that. But I don't think Cookie realized what she had. And when she did, it was too late. That's why I told her I would cover for her, not because of her, but because of you and Marquise. Deep down I was jealous, because I wish I had someone in my life like you who loved me like you loved Cookie. Last night when we were together was the first time I made love to a man since my husband. And I wanted you so bad. I wanted to feel you, and I wanted you to feel me too. I had sex with many men, but I only made love to two, and you are one of them.

"So like I said, I'm feeling love and confusion because I'm so confused about this love I feel about you."

With tears rolling down her eyes, I grabbed a tissue from the table and wiped her face.

"How do you feel about me, Jordan?" she said.

"I don't know."

"Is it because I'm a prostitute?"

"No, no, that's not it."

"Then what is it? Why won't you say?"

"Barbara, I just don't let people get close to my heart."

"Why?"

"Because the last girl I let get close, left me by myself. She walked away when I needed her most."

"Maybe that's what was wrong."

"What?"

"She was a girl and not a woman. I was told something a long time ago."

"What's that?"

"That when girls can't handle it, they run and hide. But a real woman will never leave her man's side. You can't tell me last night you didn't make love to me."

"I did, but that was a mistake," I said.

"Love is never a mistake. God is love and God is never wrong."

Looking into Barbara's beautiful brown eyes, I reached over and we began passionately kissing. I couldn't deny the feelings that were inside of me any longer. After cutting off the TV, we both started walking upstairs to Barbara's room. Then

I stopped.

"No, no, not here," I said.

"Why, what's wrong," she said, holding my hand.

"Just get your jacket," I said.

After getting our jackets, we left my mother's house and got into my car.

"Where are we going?" she asked.

"Just chill and listen to the music," I said, pulling out of the garage. "You're going with me tonight."

Turning on the radio, she reclined back in her seat and just enjoyed the ride.

Walking into my apartment thirty minutes later, the smooth soulful sound of Anita Baker was coming out of my CD player. It was a habit to leave my music playing all day long. Thank God my Uncle Paul had remembered and left it on.

The lights were already dimmed throughout my plush two-bedroom apartment. One room was for Marquise when he came over on the weekends. A few pictures of me and Marquise were on the wall mantle. My long glass coffee table was surrounded by the black leather sofa and love chair. The beige carpet was wall to wall throughout my luxurious apartment.

Grabbing Barbara's hand, she followed me into my bedroom. Entering my large room, my king size bed laid up against the wall of mirrors. My ceiling also was filled with a large mirror and four small yellow lights planted inside of them. On my dresser were all types of different lotions and deodorants. On my nightstand that was beside the bed were a few magazines, Ebony, The Source and Jet. My large TV stood on a shiny brass stand in front of my bed.

Looking into Barbara's eyes, I slowly began undressing

her. She never said a word as I took off every bit of clothes she was wearing. Standing there in front of me totally naked, I laid her on the bed.

"Why are you still dressed?" she said.

"Shhhh, just be quiet," I said, getting up, walking into the kitchen.

Walking back out with a can of whipped cream and a glass full of ice cubes; I sat them on the bed, and then got undressed. While Barbara lay there, I grabbed the can of whipped cream and squirted it on her perfect round breasts.

"Don't move," I said, as she lay there with both eyes tightly closed. Slowly I began sucking the whipped cream off her nipples.

"Ohhhh," she moaned, as I licked all of the cream off her with my traveling tongue. Grabbing an ice cube from the glass, I laid it on her navel. I could feel her body shivering with excitement. I just let it sit there as I took the can of whipped cream and started squirting it all over her breasts and pussy.

She was so excited I could see her wetness running from her pussy down to the blanket. I then sucked the whipped cream from off her breasts again. Then I started slowly sucking it off her clit. As I licked every part of her clit, I could see the lonely ice cube quickly melting from the heat that her body quickly releasing.

As I continued to massage her clitoris with my tongue, I reached over and grabbed two more ice cubes from the glass. I then took one of them and put it where the last one had melted. And the other one, I kept in my hand and rubbed it back and forth on her erected nipples.

"Ohhhh, mmmm, ahhhhh," she moaned as her entire body trembled. I then took my large middle finger and slowly entered her ass. "Ooohhhhhh," she screamed, as I turned my finger in a circular motion, while at the same time licking her clit and rubbing her breast with an ice cube. The wetness from her pussy began running down like a waterfall. Slowly tears began falling down her eyes from the sexual excitement she was experiencing. Looking up, I noticed that the second ice cube had melted too.

"Put it in, Please, I can't take it any more," she screamed.

But I wasn't in any rush. I continued to suck her clit and keep my finger in her ass until she finally had an orgasm.

"Ohhhhhh, Oh, my God! Ahhhhh, ummmm," she screamed in her loudest voice. Now I was ready to enter her. Lifting both of her legs onto my shoulders, I deeply entered her wet and vibrating pussy. Looking at her hard sexual expressions turned me on, as I repeatedly stroked in and out of her.

"Ohhh, no," I'm coming again, she said, in a crying voice. Deep inside of her, I could feel the orgasm's flow. All night we made love. All night we enjoyed the comfort of each other's body.

That wonderful night became the beginning of our future. And thanks to Mom, I didn't run away.

Chapter 16

April 28th… Tuesday afternoon…

Barbara, Steve and two other women were inside Barbara's apartment. "Don't anybody know anything?" Steve shouted. "Nothing at all?"

"Nothing, Steve. I kept calling that night after I took him the first $500 and he wouldn't pick up his cell phone, so I held all the money for you," Barbara said. "Here," she said, passing Steve a large stack of money.

"How much is this?" Steve said.

"It's $3700 from Friday night. I didn't let the girls work anymore, because RW never showed up. I didn't want to take a chance and lose any of your money. I tried calling you but I never got an answer."

"I've been having problems with my phone. I'll get that fixed. Thanks, Barbara," Steve said, putting the money in his jacket pocket. "I still don't know who would kill him like that," Steve said, shaking his head. "And why would he be parked on the small dark street, and not around people in public places like I told him."

"Maybe someone just tried to rob him," one of the girls

said.

"The news said he still had money on him, so robbery is out of the question."

"What are we going to do now?" Barbara said.

"I got to look for a replacement for RW. I'll be busy this week. I want y'all to chill for about a week. There've been too many cops around asking questions."

"The girls can stay here while I'm gone," Barbara said.

"Where are you going?" Steve asked.

"I'm going over to my sister's to be with my son."

"Okay. I'll call you, Barbara, when I get this shit back in order."

Barbara and the other women all walked upstairs.

"Why the hell was RW on that street?" Steve said to himself as he walked out the door. Looking out the window from the second floor, the women all smiled, as Steve got into his Lexus and drove off.

"Soon it will be all over with girls," Barbara said, hugging each one of them.

After Steve drove off, Barbara immediately called me from her cell phone.

"Hello," I said, lying across my bed half dressed.

"He just left."

"Oh, yeah, what did he say?"

"He told us to chill out for about a week. He's looking for someone to take RW's place."

"That's good news," I said.

"I gave him the money you gave me to give him. And I told all the girls to keep the money they made Friday, Saturday, Sunday and last night.

"That's good. Are the girls happy?"

"Damn right! They all have over a thousand dollars a piece. I told Steve we only worked on Friday and he went for it. What are you about to do now?"

"I'm waiting for my uncle and Chico to come over. They just called me and said they'll be here soon."

"Okay. I have a few things to do with the girls. I'll be over later tonight."

"What do you have to do?"

"We're meeting your mother in a few hours."

"Oh, yeah, that's right. My mother told me she's meeting with you and the girls today."

"So I'll see you later. I have the keys you gave me."

"Okay, Barb, I'll see you later tonight," I said, hanging up the phone.

Uncle Paul and Chico walked into my bedroom with large bags in their hands.

"Where y'all been for the last couple of days?" I said.

"Atlantic City, New York and Baltimore," Chico said, smiling.

"*What*! With who?"

"The twins, that's who," Chico said.

"First we went to Atlantic City, then we drove to New York," Uncle Paul said. "Then I said fuck it, we've been enjoying ourselves all weekend. Let's go to Baltimore to hang-out and eat crabs."

"That's why we didn't come back on Monday," Chico said interrupting.

"The twins were from New York. They took us around town and we stayed over at their Manhattan apartment," Uncle Paul said.

"How was your weekend?" Chico said.

"Special," I answered.

"Special?" Uncle Paul and Chico said at the same time.

"Yeah, I met a new friend too."

"Who, some chick from the party?" Uncle Paul said.

"No, Barbara," I said.

"Barbara!" Chico said.

"Yeah, Barbara. And she is something *special*," I said smiling.

"She is fine ass shit," Chico said.

"So what's up with y'all?" Uncle Paul asked.

"Just taking things one day at a time, that's all."

"I saw the way you two looked at each other," Chico said smiling. "Pay up, Paul."

"I told him y'all liked each other and something was going to happen."

"Y'all two had a bet?" I said.

"Yeah, $100," Uncle Paul said, going into his pants pockets, pulling out a large stack of hundred dollar bills, passing one of them to Chico.

"I can tell when two people like each other," Chico said, counting his money.

"What's in the bags?"

"Souvenirs," Chico said.

"I have some New York T-shirts, Atlantic City T-shirts, furry dice and some stuff we picked up in Baltimore. I have to be back in California tonight, that's why we came back today."

"Why? What's up?" I said.

"Tonight we got that shipment coming through. Back to business," Chico said.

"The guy Steve is back in town," I said.

"Oh, yeah," Uncle Paul said.

"Yeah. Next week we'll take care of that chump," I said.

"I'll be back next week too," Chico said. "Business should be back in order by then."

"I got a box of new 9-millimeters that just came in," Uncle Paul said, smiling.

"That nigga will pay for what he did to Cookie," I said.

"Don't do anything stupid," Chico said, putting his hand on my shoulder.

"The way I feel, I could kill him in broad daylight," I said.

"Stick to the plan, Jordan. We'll let Barbara set it up. Just like we planned," Uncle Paul said.

"Yeah, you got too much to lose now. We've got to do everything right," Chico said.

"I'm tired, Jordan. I'm going over to Paul's to take a nap before I catch my plane tonight."

"We'll see you later," Uncle Paul said, walking out of my room.

"I'll be by there to take you to the airport later. I have to go get my son from school in a few hours."

"Okay, later," Uncle Paul said, as he and Chico walked out the door.

Looking at the clock on my bedroom wall, I noticed the time was one o'clock. After taking a shower, I got dressed and drove to a Wendy's restaurant to get something to eat. I then got my car washed and went to pick up Marquise from school before 3 o'clock when he got released.

That afternoon, inside his yacht...

"Everything is alright," Sid said, talking to Pedro on the phone. "It just got through. I'm in the warehouse now."

"Everything?" Pedro said, lying on his bed with Mia

naked beside him.

"Everything. No problems this time."

"Okay. I'll see you later. I'm on my way home with Mia. I'll talk to you, Sid," Pedro said.

"So you can't stay just a little bit longer, baby?"

"I have to take my mother to see her doctor, honey. Next time, I promise," Mia said, kissing Pedro on his chest.

"Okay, okay, I'll take you home."

"Are we still going out to dinner tonight?" Mia asked, putting on her clothes.

"Yes. When you come back from your mother's house, I'll be waiting. I'm surprised you wanted to go out tonight. You've been so tired lately from helping your mother so much."

"Tonight, I just want to be with you. Nothing can keep me away from you tonight, honey," Mia said, smiling.

"I'll be waiting, my love," Pedro said.

"Me too," Mia smiled. "Me too."

On a small deserted street in South Central L.A...

Inside his police car, Tucker and Mr. Lee were talking.

"I'll have everything ready for you in a few days."

"3000 kilos," the man said.

"Yeah, but first I've got to get rid of a few problems, then everything should be okay."

"The same price, right?"

"Four thousand a key, ain't nothing changed. Just like last time."

"I'll have your money ready," the man said.

"Just give me a few days, Lee, and I'll meet you again at

your office in Chinatown."

"Okay, Tucker, I'll talk with you soon," Lee said, getting out of the car.

Turning on his police siren, Tucker quickly sped down the street and disappeared.

Walking across the street, Lee got into a waiting black limousine. The driver then pulled off in the opposite direction.

Driving on the expressway with Marquise inside the car, I noticed a sad look on his face. "What's wrong, buddy?"

"Nothing, Dad," he said, with both arms folded, looking straight ahead.

"Something is wrong. What is it?"

"It's school."

"What about school," I said.

"The kids were teasing me today."

"About what?"

"About my mommy."

"What did the kids say?"

"They said my mommy was on drugs."

"They did!" I said in a surprised voice.

"Yes, and they said that's why she got shot. Dad, did my mommy get shot?"

"Your mommy is in heaven. Don't listen to them."

"Please, Daddy, tell me. Did my mom get shot and die?"

"Yes, Marquise, your mommy got shot. I didn't want to tell you, but that's what happened to her."

"Did they leave my mommy in the trashcan?"

"No. Now that's it. We're not going to talk about it anymore," I said, turning up the radio.

I never wanted to tell Marquise the truth about his mother's death, but I knew one day he would find out. Looking over at him while I drove, I could see a look of pain and anger all on his little face. Something was bothering him, something deep down inside. I felt so sad for my son and what his mother had taken him through at such an early age. Pulling into my mother's driveway, Marquise's expression never changed. They say, "Time heals all wounds." I don't think Marquise's pain will ever heal. The loss of his mother will be something that my young son will live with forever, and eventually take to his grave.

Chapter 17

Santa Monica, California...

Mia had just left to go over to her mother's house. Pedro and Sid were both inside the living room talking.

"The shipment came early today," Sid said.

"Yeah, Tucker thought it would be better to switch the time a little earlier. So I agreed."

"The men are packing the arcades now, getting them ready for distribution."

"Good, now everything is back in order. I already paid my supplier his money and told him that we will not have anymore setbacks like that anymore?"

"Everything will be ready to go out on Friday," Sid said.

"I'm expecting Chico home tonight," Pedro said, sitting on the couch noticing the large yellow envelope sitting on top of the glass coffee table with the words, "Private documents" written on it.

Picking up the large envelope, Pedro called Ruiz.

"Ruiz, Ruiz," Pedro said.

"Yes, Pedro," Ruiz said, walking down the stairs.

"What's this?" he said, showing him the large envelope.

"Oh, a man dropped it off yesterday for Chico."

"What was the man's name?"

"His name was Tom. He just said it was for Chico and left."

"Did he say what it was?"

"No, but Chico did call me and told me that if it came to put it up."

"Here, I'll ask him about it tonight when he gets back from Philly. Put it in his bedroom," Pedro said, passing it to Ruiz.

Taking the envelope, Ruiz walked back upstairs and set it on Chico's bed.

Long Beach, California...

In a small hotel room, Tucker and Mia had just finished making love. "Everything is all set. Tonight is the night," Tucker said, kissing around Mia's breast. "Once Pedro is out of the way, then it's Chico and Sid next. I'll be the only one left to run things."

"Don't you mean, me and you?" Mia smiled.

"Yeah, you know that's what I meant. I talked to my buyer today. He said he's ready and the money is waiting. Three thousand a kilo, and you and I will split everything, my love."

Lying across the bed, Mia continued to smile.

"Are you ready for tonight?"

"Yes, baby, I'm ready," she said.

"Everything is set. It's now up to you."

"He'll be there. I told him I wanted to go out tonight. Knowing him, he's probably waiting for me now. Believe me, he'll break his neck to be there for his Mia."

Grabbing Mia in his arms, Tucker began kissing her

around her neck.

"Ohhhh, baby, that feels so good. I can't wait till we don't have to hide our love anymore," she said.

"It's all up to you, beautiful. The ball is in your corner now."

"I'll take care of everything. You'll be proud of me, I promise. Then we can kill Chico," Mia said.

"Yes, honey, then we will kill Chico."

Laying Mia on her back, Tucker began making love to her once again.

Philadelphia, PA...

Inside Uncle Paul's apartment in West Philly, I watched as he and Chico were playing an intense game of chess.

"Checkmate!" Chico yelled out.

"That's four straight Unc, you're getting over there," I said.

"I have to admit you got a hellava game Chico," Uncle Paul said, putting the chessboard and pieces away.

"I was taught by the best," Chico smilingly said.

"Who? Bobby Fisher?" Uncle Paul said, as he walked towards the bedroom

"Nope, Jordan showed."

"Man, I must be losing my game, cause I showed Jordan how to play."

"Next time I'll take it easy on you," Chico said, as he and I started laughing.

Uncle Paul came out of the bedroom holding a box in his hand. "Here they are," he said, opening the box.

Inside were six brand new black 9-millimeter handguns.

"Do you need any, Jordan?"

"No, not right now. I still have two that are not used. One right here," I said, lifting up my t-shirt. "And the one I always keep inside my glove compartment."

"I wish I could take one back with me to Cali," Chico said, seeing them inside the box.

"I got them for $300 a piece," Uncle Paul smiled.

"You could sell each of these for six or seven hundred in L.A."

Chico noticed the time on his platinum Rolex watch "It's eight-fifteen my plane leaves in two hours. Let me go get dressed," he said, getting up and walking into the other room.

"Yeah, it's getting late," Uncle Paul said, looking at his platinum Rolex too. "I have some things to do myself," he said, closing the box. "Chico, I'll see you next week," he hollered, walking out the door holding the box of guns in his hand.

"He left out. He said he'd see you next week."

"Oh, I didn't hear him. I'll be one minute," Chico said, going into the bathroom.

As I sat in a chair waiting for Chico, the thought of Marquise entered my mind. His sadness had upset me. The more I thought of the pain he was going through, the more I wanted to kill Steve for what he had done to my son.

Turning on the TV, I waited for Chico to get washed and dressed so I could take him to catch his plane back to California.

"Hello," Pedro said, answering his telephone.

"Baby, it's me."

"Where are you? I've been waiting."

"I'm stuck. My car broke down on the side of the road,"

Mia said, crying. "I'm scared. There's no one out here but me."

"I'm on my way. Where are you?"

"I'm on Eighty-seventh Street in South Central. When I left my mother's I went to see some old friends and on my way back home, this damn car shut off again. Please hurry up. I'm afraid out here."

"Okay. I'll try and call Tucker first. That's his district. But I'm still on my way."

"Okay, hurry up, baby, cuz my battery in my cell is running out too."

Mia's phone suddenly went dead leaving Pedro's phone with only a dial tone.

Pedro quickly dialed Tucker on his cell phone. After two rings, Tucker answered his phone.

"Hello," Tucker said.

"Tuck, where are you?"

"I'm at the community meeting with my sergeant and captain."

"Oh, shit! That's right. You told me about that."

"Why? What's up?"

"Mia's car broke down on 87th Street. She's out there alone."

"Well, I can call someone and tell them to go make sure she's okay."

"Thanks, Tuck, I'm on my way to go get her now. I'll call her and tell her that someone's on their way, to stay calm."

"Okay, Pedro, I'll do it now. But you better hurry up. It's getting dark out."

"Bye, Tuck," Pedro said, hanging up the phone.

Dialing Mia back on her cell phone, the voice mail came

on.

"Damn! The battery must have died," Pedro said, rushing out the door.

Getting inside of his Porsche, Pedro quickly sped out of the garage.

After dropping Chico off at the airport to catch his plane back to California, I drove to my apartment. Entering my apartment, the smell of good home cooking filled the air. Walking into the kitchen, Barbara was standing there in some sexy black lingerie. Her long black hair laid down her back, showing her entire beautiful face. Under her lingerie, I could see her perfect breasts. On the decorated table were a bottle of red wine and two plates. On each plate was a large piece of sirloin steak, mashed potatoes and steamed string beans. The only light was from three small candles that were burning around the large table. The CD player had the smooth sounds of Teddy Pendergrass flowing from its speakers. Looking at the clock on the wall, I noticed the time was now 10:27.

"What took you so long?" Barbara said, walking up to me giving me a long passionate kiss. "I had to drop Chico off, remember?"

"Well, the food is still nice and warm. Are you hungry?"

"I'm starving," I said, looking at all the home cooked food on the table.

"Hold up. First you have to go change," Barbara said, smiling.

"Change!" I said.

"Yeah, I bought you something to put on. It's on the bed."

"Hurry up. I'll be waiting," she said, taking a seat at the table.

I walked into my bedroom and saw the black silk Gucci underwear on my bed. I put it on and walked back into the kitchen.

"Now that's what I'm talking about," Barbara said, looking at me standing there in just the black silk shorts.

"I can eat a horse right now," I said, taking a seat at the table.

Getting up from her chair and walking over to me, Barbara got on both of her knees. "I can eat a horse right now too," she said, going into my underwear, pulling out my dick. "You don't mind if I have an appetizer before dinner do you?" she said, holding my now hard dick in her hands.

"Not at all," I said, as she gently placed her warm lips around the head of my dick and began eating me, like a full course meal.

"Let me talk to Pedro," Chico said, talking on his cell phone, looking out the window of the plane.

"He left a while ago," Ruiz said.

"Do you know where he went?" Chico said.

"No, he just ran out, leaving his jacket and cell phone on the couch."

"Damn! What could have been so important?"

"He didn't say. He just ran to the garage and got into his Porsche."

"I'll be there in a few hours," Chico said.

"Oh, Chico!" Ruiz said.

"What Ruiz?"

"Your mail was dropped off yesterday."

"What mail?"

"From a Tom Leavy."

"Oh, yeah. I almost forgot. Where is it?"

"It's on your bed. Pedro had it."

"Did he look at it?"

"No, he never opened it."

"Okay, good. I'll look at it in the morning. Tonight I'm just coming home and going to bed. If Pedro comes back home, tell him I called."

"I certainly will, Chico. Anything else?"

"No, that's it. I'm about to take a quick nap now. Bye, Ruiz," Chico said, hanging up his cell phone. Tucking a small pillow behind his neck, he reclined his chair and closed his eyes, as he thought about the wonderful weekend he spent with the lovely twins.

In his white Porsche, Pedro spotted Mia's Lexus double parked on the side of the road. The sky was pitch black on this moonless Tuesday night, as he quickly pulled behind her disabled car.

Getting out of his car, holding a small flashlight, he saw Mia sitting inside her Lexus. With the doors locked and the windows all rolled up, the hood of the car was also up, as Pedro walked up to the car and tapped on the window, noticing Mia on her cell phone.

Mia then got out of the car with the phone still to her ear. "I'm on the phone with the tow truck people," she said, hugging Pedro. "My boyfriend is here now," she said, walking to the front of the car with Pedro.

Looking under the hood of the car, Pedro searched to see what was wrong.

"He's checking it out now. Hurry up," she said, looking around.

"I think it might be a blown gasket or something," Pedro said, bent over with his flashlight in his hand. Pulling up behind Pedro's Porsche, a flashing police car parked.

"Who's that?" Pedro asked, with his head still under the hood.

"It's a police car," she said, finally closing her cell phone.

"Oh, Tucker told me that he would send someone over," Pedro said, still with his head under the hood of the car. "Mia, I thought your battery in your cell phone died," Pedro said, to no reply. "Mia, Mia," he said as he finally looked up, staring down the barrel of a 357 magnum. "Tucker, what!" were his final words before the explosive impact of the powerful slugs splattered pieces of his brain on the front of the car and his lifeless body slumped to the cold earth where so many others had become victims too. Folding his cell phone that was in his other hand, Tucker looked at Mia who was now sitting behind the driver's seat of her car. Reaching down in the engine, he grabbed the unattached red positive plug to the car's battery and screwed it back on. After closing the hood of the car, Tucker stepped over Pedro's deceased corpse. "Get out of here now," he said, as Mia started up her car, backed up and drove down the street disappearing into the black night. Getting back into his police car, Tucker made a sudden U-turn and quickly drove away, leaving Pedro's dead and mangled body on the side of the road, a few feet away from his Porsche.

Chapter 18

The sound of the loud doorbell rang in the late hours of the night, as Chico was sound asleep in the comfort of his warm bed. Hearing the loud bell, Ruiz got up to answer the door. Walking down the stairs, Ruiz could see two white men standing out in front of the door. Instantly Ruiz recognized that they were cops. Ruiz quickly opened the door. "Yes, can I help you," he said.

"Hi, my name is Detective Knight," one of the men said, holding a badge in his hand.

"And my name is Detective Jackson," the other one said.

"What's wrong, sir," Ruiz asked.

"We found a body we believe to be that of Mr. Pedro Chiccaro. He was shot in South Central L.A. He was shot twice in the head, a few feet away from his car and left on the side of the road," Detective Knight said.

"What! Pedro is dead!" Ruiz said, shaking his head in disbelief. "No! Not Pedro!" he said.

"Are you a relative, sir?" Detective Jackson asked.

"No, I just work for him. His brother is upstairs sleeping."

"Well could you please wake him up? We need a relative

to identify the body."

"I don't believe this!" Ruiz said, walking up the stairs.

Outside of Chico's bedroom, Ruiz banged on the door. Getting up, Chico opened his door.

"Ruiz, Ruiz, what is the problem," Chico said, still half asleep.

"Sir, I have some very bad news," he said.

"What is it, Ruiz, that's so important it couldn't wait to the morning?"

"Your brother has been murdered."

"What! What are you talking about? Who told you this?"

"The detectives are at the door, sir."

Quickly running down the stairs, Ruiz followed Chico to the door.

"Oh, no, please! Please God!" Chico hollered, seeing the two waiting officers outside his door. "Is this true? Is Pedro dead?" he cried out.

"Yes, Mr. Chiccaro, your brother was shot and killed earlier today" Detective Knight said.

"Are you sure it's Pedro?" Chico said, with a flow of tears falling from his tearful face.

"Does your brother drive a 1997 white Porsche?"

"No, no! No! Pedro! God why! Why Pedro!" Chico said, falling to his knees. "Ahhhh," Chico screamed out, as it echoed off all the walls.

"Would you mind getting dressed and going down to the coroner's to identify the body, sir?" Detective Jackson said, putting his arm around Chico.

"No! Pedro! Pedro! Pedro! Do you know who killed him?" Chico said, standing up with the look of a confused madman.

"No, sir, right now we have little clues to go on," Detective Knight said.

Walking downstairs in a red silk robe, Mia saw Chico on his knees crying. "Chico, what's wrong?" she said, walking over to him.

"Pedro is dead! Somebody killed my brother!" he yelled.

"No, not my Pedro!" she screamed, putting on an act that could have easily won her the best actress award. "Oh, my God! My fiancé is dead!" she cried out.

"Why wasn't he home?" Chico said, standing to his feet.

"He told me that he was going to the yacht tonight," Mia said, sitting down, crying on the couch. "Oh, I don't believe he is gone. My Pedro! My love! Why this! Why my sweet Pedro!" Mia cried out. "What happened?" she said. "Tell me what happened!"

"He was shot, and his body dumped on the side of the road," Detective Jackson said.

"Where? Where at?" Mia asked.

"In South Central L.A.," Detective Knight said.

"What was he doing in South Central?" Chico said.

"Right now we don't know if he was taken there or went on his own," Detective Knight said. "There have been a number of carjackings recently around the city," Detective Jackson said.

"No! Why Pedro. How could someone kill Pedro," Mia said, with her head on Ruiz' shoulder.

"I'm sorry, Ma'am. I'm so sorry," Detective Knight said.

"Please forgive us for disturbing y'all tonight with this very upsetting news. We'll be outside waiting to take you both downtown. We'll need y'all to answer a few questions at headquarters, if you don't mind," Detective Jackson said, as he and his partner walked out the door.

Chico sat at the bottom of the steps with his head down. All he could do was cry. Dealing with the reality that Pedro was dead and there was no way he could bring his brother back.

Thursday, April 2nd...

Two days later...after catching a flight to California, Chico, Tucker, Sid and I were all sitting in the living room talking. Mia had just left to go handle some arrangements for Pedro's funeral with Ruiz.

"Tucker, is there any way you can find out anything about Pedro's death?"

"I've been on it for two days, Chico. Nothing! Not one clue. As soon as I find out anything, you'll be the first to know," Tucker said.

"The funeral is Saturday. He'll be buried next to our mother," Chico said.

"What's that, Chico," Tucker said, pointing to a piece of paper that Chico had.

"It's Pedro's will."

"Pedro had a will?" Sid said.

"Yes, he had it done up months ago by his lawyers. Just in case anything happened to him."

"What does it say," I said, looking across the table at his sad face.

"He left everything to me...and Mia."

"Mia!" Tucker said, with a smirk on his face.

"Yeah, the house, the cars, the yacht, the jewels. And the money."

"How much money?" Tucker asked.

Chico paused, looked around the table at all four of our

faces, then said, "All together, in banks, off shore accounts, investments, stocks and bonds..."

"How much?" Tucker interrupted again, with the look of a hungry lion on his face.

"One hundred million dollars!"

"What! One hundred million bucks," Tucker said.

"Whoa! Mia gets half," Sid said, shaking his head.

"Half. She gets half of everything!" Chico said.

"I just wanted to let everyone know that nothing's changed. Business must still go on. Tucker, you and Sid will be running the shipments making sure everyone is taken care of. After the funeral on Saturday, I'm taking a vacation for awhile."

"What about Mia, does she know?" Tucker said.

"Yes, Mia had already been told. The lawyers told us both earlier today."

"Did the will say anything else?" Sid asked.

"Yes, it said that if Mia or myself died, the other would automatically take over everything and have a hundred percent control."

"Do you think Mia can handle all of this sudden income?" I asked.

"I'll have to teach her. That's what Pedro would want," Chico said.

"Who's Jaguar is that in the garage?" Tucker asked.

"It's Mia's. Pedro was going to surprise her yesterday."

"Damn! Pedro really loved that woman," Sid said, shaking his head.

"Okay, fellas, everything will be back to basics after Pedro's funeral. Any questions?"

No one said a word, as everyone stood up from the table

and hugged and shook hands. The four of us then walked to the front door.

"I'll see you Saturday," Tucker said, walking outside getting into his Range Rover and driving away.

"I'll call you later," Sid said, getting into his Chevy Tahoe LS and following Tucker down the path and out the gate.

Chico and I then walked upstairs into his room, where the two of us took a seat on the bed and started sorting out some of Pedro's belongings.

"Are you okay?" I said, seeing the noticeable pain inside his watery eyes.

"I'm fine. I have to be. It's just me now," Chico said, looking through all the papers.

"And me," I said, as he looked up and finally showed a smile on his face.

"I don't believe he's gone, first my mother, now my brother."

"You still have one brother," I said, picking up a large yellow envelope that was laying on the bed. "What's this?" I asked.

"Oh, I forgot about that. It's been here since Monday."

"What is it?"

"It's from my friend, Tom."

"Who?"

"The private investigator."

"Oh, yeah, you told me. You never checked?"

"No, I've been too busy the last few days. I almost forgot about it."

Tearing the seal off, Chico opened the envelope and pulled out a large stack of 8x10 black and white photos with a cover letter on top of them.

"Dear Chico, Inside is the information that you requested. All receipts and other signed documents between us have been destroyed like you asked me to do. I hope you enjoy.

Tom Leavy,
LA #1 Private Eye"

After reading Tom's letter, Chico looked at the first photo. The photo was of Mia getting out of her Lexus outside of a nail salon. The next few photos showed Mia walking out of a hair salon and a jewelry store. Then all of the photos quickly changed. The next two photos showed Mia going into a Beverly Hills Hotel with a blond wig and dark shades on. We both stayed silent as we continued to look through the rest of the photos. The next photo was of Tucker in his police uniform walking into the same hotel. The next photo was Mia again, this time in a red wig and shades going into another hotel. The next one was Tucker going into the same hotel moments later. We knew because the time and date that each picture was taken were on the bottom of each photo. The next 10 photos were all the same. Mia going into different hotels and moments later, Tucker was right behind her. Each time Mia had a different wig on. Chico then looked at one of the photos and noticed a day and time when Mia said she was over her mother's house. "That whore! That tramp was playing my brother! I told him about that slut! That no good trash."

We both knew what was going on now. Mia was having an affair with Tucker.

"Them two set up Pedro!" Chico said, ripping that photo in half. That's why my brother was found in Tucker's district. Hold on Chico said, running out of the room. A few moments later Chico returned back to the room.

"What's up? Where did you go?"

"I went to check the caller ID box," Chico sadly said.

"What did it say?"

"Mia had called the house right before Pedro was murdered, something made him hurry up and leave the house that night."

"What do you think it was?"

"It don't matter, Pedro would break his neck for Mia, no matter what it was."

"So she got him out of the house huh?"

"Yeah, she set my brother up and Tucker was in on it, because the caller ID box had his number on it too."

"He called?"

"No, Pedro called him, so something big must have happened that night, that bitch! These two have been setting us the fuck up!"

"Calm down, Chico," I said, looking into his vengeful eyes.

"They will pay for what the did to Pedro. They will both wish they never crossed us. I put that on my mother's grave. That's why Tucker couldn't be there with Sid when the shipments came through. He's always there. That's why Mia came in the other night and went straight to bed. Not once did she ask about Pedro that night."

"But didn't she say that Pedro was at his boat?"

"Pedro would never have gone to his yacht knowing I was coming home. We always discuss business first."

"You think they set him up?"

"Yes, I'm positive. I know they did."

"Why? Why would they?"

"Greed! It's always greed! Tucker probably wasn't satisfied with the hundred and fifty kilos we gave him for every shipment that he got through."

"What about Mia?"

"That whore wanted it all! The house, cars, everything. I told Pedro she never loved him. I told him so many times. I should have kicked that bitch out the first time she ..." Chico paused and put his head down.

"She what?" I asked.

"She came into my room when Pedro was away on a business trip."

"What! You and Mia?"

"Once. I regret it. It was when he had first met her. I had no idea that she would one day become his fiancé. Pedro and I shared plenty of women before. Afterwards, I felt bad and told her that I was sorry. She belonged to my brother. And that was it. Pedro never found out."

"Oh, shit! Damn Chico! You fucked your brother's fiancé?"

"She wasn't his fiancé at the time. But that's not all."

"There's more?"

"Plenty more. After we made love that night, a few weeks later she found out that she was pregnant with my child."

"Oh, my God!" I said, shaking my head.

"Though she wanted to keep it, I convinced her to get rid of it. Pedro would never have forgiven me for that. Never! She cried, but I told her she must get rid of it. And soon."

"How do you know it was yours?"

"The day we made love matched up, the doctor said. She wanted to continue the one-time affair. She begged me. But I told her that was it for us. That if she kept it up I would tell

Pedro and she would surely be cut off. She knew I was serious then."

"Oh, wow! This is crazy," I said.

"That's why she never loved Pedro. That's why."

"Why's that?"

"Because she's always been in love with me. She never loved Pedro, and she knew she could never have me. So she ran into the arms of another...Tucker."

"Does anyone else know about you and Mia's affair?"

"Only Ruiz."

"Ruiz knows?"

"Yes. That night he saw Mia sneak out of my bedroom back into Pedro's. We talked and he promised not to say anything to Pedro. I told him that it would never happen again. And he believed me. That's why I know they both set my brother up. They are both snakes! Two fucking snakes! They deserve to be together—the cobra and the rattlesnake. Two of man's most feared enemies. There's only one way to take care of snakes."

"How?"

"You feed them to sharks."

"What?"

"You heard me. You feed them to sharks."

"What are you talking about, Chico?"

"You'll find out, Jordan. After the funeral Saturday, you'll understand."

After putting everything inside a small box that was on the floor, Chico and I walked out of the room. I did not understand what he was talking about, but soon I would find out.

Chapter 19

Friday afternoon...

Inside a hotel room in Beverly Hills, Tucker and Mia once again had just finished making love.

"Once Chico is dead we'll have the whole $100 million," Tucker said.

"Why can't we kill him now, like we did Pedro?"

"Let things calm down first. Then we'll kill 'em."

"I want him dead, Tucker. I want Chico dead now!"

"I said we'd wait, Mia. Why is killing Chico so important to you?"

"I just hate him. I hate his ass!"

"Is there something you're not telling me, Mia?"

"No, baby, I just think he'll eventually become a bigger problem than Pedro was. We just don't need him around. He deserves to die for all of the innocent people he killed."

"What are you talking about? Chico never killed anybody."

"He killed an innocent helpless child before."

"How do you know? Who told you?"

"I know, because Pedro told me, that's how."

"Well stop worrying. He'll soon be dead and we'll be a whole lot richer," Tucker said, smiling. "One hundred million dollars richer. Next week my Chinese buyer wants to buy 3000 kilos. Chico will be dead before the next shipment arrives. I promise."

Sitting up on the bed in her naked body, Mia grabbed an opened bottle of champagne from off the dresser. Slowly pouring it over her head, it traveled down her perfectly round breasts, wetting her entire body with a sexy look on her beautiful face. "Fuck me, Tucker," she yelled out. "Come fuck me. Tell me you love me, Tucker. Let me hear it."

"I love you, Mia," Tucker said, reaching over grabbing Mia's soaking wet body. Laying her back down on the wet bed, Tucker and Mia began making love again, in the small private room and in a $300 dollar bottle of champagne.

"I'll be home next week, baby," I said, talking to Barbara on the phone.

"I miss you so much, Jordan."

"I just have to be here for my friend. He's like my brother."

"I understand. The boys are over here keeping me company. I picked them up after school. It's Friday. They can both hang up with me tonight. There's no school tomorrow."

"Make sure they don't break anything. Marquise likes to touch things."

"I will."

"Did you talk to Steve?"

"He called me."

"What did he say?"

"He just said to be ready by next week. That he would have a replacement to take RW's place."

"Okay, that's cool. Where's Marquise?"

"He's right here next to me."

"Put him on."

"Hi, Daddy."

"What's up, buddy?"

"Is Uncle Chico alright?"

"Yes, Uncle Chico is fine. Have you been good?"

"Yes. And I did what you told me to do and told the teacher when the other kids mess with me."

"Okay, good boy. I'm proud of you. Next Thursday is your birthday. You'll be eight years old. Are you ready?"

"Yes, I'm tired of being seven. Can we do something special on my birthday? Just you and me, Daddy, please."

"What do you want to do, buddy? You name it, anything."

"I want to go to the movies. Then I want a new bike. Then can you take me to see my mommy's grave?"

"You want to go see your mother's grave?"

"Yes, Daddy. I got something important to tell her."

"What?"

"Daddy, it's a secret," Marquise said.

"Yes, Marquise, I'll take you by your mother's grave."

"Thanks, Daddy. Thank you so much. I love you."

"I love you too. Now put Barbara back on the phone."

"Hello," Barbara said, getting back on the phone.

"You heard him?"

"Yes, I heard him. You should see the smile on his face. I think it will be fine. He misses his mother."

"What does he mean he has something to tell her?"

"I don't know, but he said it to me too."

"He did?"

"Yeah, earlier today. You know how kids are."

"Yeah, but Marquise is different."

"Well, it won't hurt to take him to see his mother's grave."

"How was dinner the other night?"

"Perfect. Just as good as Mom's."

"That's who gave me the recipe."

"On how to cook a steak?"

"No, on how to satisfy a man. First you eat 'em, then you feed 'em, and then you please him."

"Who told you that?" I said, smiling.

"Your mom. You were right. She is cool as shit," Barbara said, laughing into the phone.

"I'm going to have to have a talk with my mom. She's got issues."

"You just hurry up back here and let me release some of that tension."

"I'll be home soon. Tell Marquise I love him."

"He's in the room with Sharrod now, but I'll tell him."

"Bye, Barbara. I'll call you back later."

"Bye, Jordan," she said, hanging up the phone.

That Saturday afternoon, at the God's Angels cemetery in San Diego, California, Chico and I stood side by side and watched Pedro's body finally exit this cruel and harsh world that we live in. The weather was at peace on this mournful day.

Chico stood there with a confused look on his face watching the earth slowly swallow the all-white casket, with 24 karat gold trimmings around its border into this place of no return.

Mia stood there, a few feet away from us, holding a rose in her hand, as her tears fell to the ground. Tucker wasn't too far behind, as he and Sid, both dressed in all black Versace suits couldn't help but shed a few tears as well. Ruiz waited inside the black Mercedes Benz stretch limousine for Chico, Mia and me to say our final goodbyes. Dozens of white roses lay all around the casket. A few feet away, their mother's remains were in a grave where her first child would become her new neighbor.

I stood there thinking, "Here goes another young man, dead before he's thirty years old." In this fast world we all live in, once we decide to slow down, it's usually too late. Looking over at Mia, I couldn't help but wonder what she was thinking. How could she stand there and cry a river of false tears. How can a woman so beautiful be so ugly? Looking over at Tucker, I could see the greed that hid behind his fake emotions. I felt bad for Chico. He had lost his mother and his brother and never knew his forsaken father. Still only a young man, Chico had lived an old life. He was now alone in this uncertain world. In a heartbeat, he would give up every penny he had in return for his two deceased relatives. But deep down inside, I think he'd rather join them and be right by their sides.

As everyone began to leave, I put my arm around Chico to somewhat comfort his grief. Getting inside the waiting limousine, where Mia was already sitting, we pulled off and all headed back home. Tucker and Sid followed down the long dusty road of the God's Angels cemetery.

After returning back home, everyone had parked in the garage. I ran upstairs to change into some shorts, my new pair of Jordan sneakers and a T-shirt. Sid and Tucker were by the pool having a conversation with Ruiz while Mia and Chico were talking, standing by her new Jaguar.

"I miss him already, Chico," Mia cried. "I don't know what to do now," she said, looking into Chico's distant eyes.

"This is the new car that he just bought you?" Chico said.

"I told him I didn't need another car, but you know Pedro insisted. I'll cherish this last gift from him forever. I have to go soon. I promised my mother I'd visit her today. Plus I just need to get away for awhile."

"Me too," Tucker said, walking up putting his arms around Chico's shoulders. "I have a meeting in Chinatown with an important friend of mine this evening."

Ruiz and Sid both went inside, moments later returned back out.

"Before y'all leave, I have something to show y'all," Chico said.

"What is it?" Mia asked.

"I'll be right back. Give me a minute," Chico said, walking inside the house.

With the large yellow envelope in his hand, Chico walked back out. "Here, Mia," Chico said, passing the envelope to Mia and backing away standing next to me.

Opening up the large yellow envelope, Mia pulled out the stack of photos inside. Standing next to her, Tucker read a piece of paper that was on top.

"Psalm 55:15: Let death take my enemies by surprise;
                    Let them go down alive to the grave,
                    For evil finds lodging among them."

After reading the paper, Mia and Tucker began looking at all the photos.

"Oh, my God!" Mia screamed out loud. "No! No!"

"Chico, let me explain," Tucker said, dropping all the photos to the ground.

Sid and Ruiz quickly pulled out Berretta nine-millimeters

with attached silencers.

"Chico! Chico! Please, Tucker made me do it! He killed Pedro!"

"You bitch! That whore is lying, Chico. Let me explain. She wanted your brother's money," Tucker said in a scared and timid voice.

"Stop lying, you coward! You set everything up!" Mia yelled. "Chico, please, believe me. You know I still love you. You know I would never do anything to hurt you. Even after I had the abortion I still loved you. Please, Chico, Pease believe me."

"It was Chico you were talking about that you once loved. It was him who you said killed the innocent child. Oh shit! You dirty backstabbing slut!" Tucker yelled.

"Shut the fuck up! Both of y'all!" Chico said, pulling another black berretta from under his shirt.

For a moment everything became silent.

"Unlike what the two of y'all did to my brother, I'll give y'all both a chance to save your own lives."

"What! What are you talking about, Chico?" Tucker said, in a surprised voice.

"You heard me. I will spare both of your lives on one condition."

"What! Anything," Mia said.

"That Tucker, you play Jordan in a one-on-one basketball game, the best two out of three. Each game goes to 10."

"What! Are you serious?" Tucker said.

"Yes, I'm serious. If you win, I want you and this bitch to leave L.A. forever and never return. But if you lose, the two of you will both be killed."

"Chico, please, look…" Tucker said.

"Mother fucker, you killed my brother. And you were fucking his fiancé. I should kill you right now," Chico said, pointing his gun at Tucker's head. "So what are you going to do?"

"Yes, I'll play Jordan, but my shorts and stuff are inside my trunk."

"Ruiz, get this no-good mother fucka's stuff from his trunk."

Going into the pockets, Tucker threw Ruiz the keys to his Range Rover. Walking back from the garage, Ruiz had a large white Nike sports bag in one hand and a large black briefcase in the other.

"This was also in the trunk, Chico," Ruiz said, dropping Tucker's sports bag by his side and passing the briefcase to Chico.

"What's this?" Chico said, looking at Tucker.

Tucker remained silent as Chico opened the briefcase.

Opening it up, neat stacks of new hundred dollar bills were laying inside. "Whoa! Somebody hit the jackpot!" Chico said.

Chico then pulled out a small piece of paper that was inside and read it. "3000 K plus 4G each equals 12 mil."

"It was *you* who stole the cocaine?" Chico said. "This is what it's all about? Money! You killed my brother over *money*! So you were robbing us to sell kilos for $4,000 a piece?"

"You fucking greedy bastard, Tucker," Mia yelled out.

"Is this the 12 million you made?"

"Yes, it's all there, every penny," Tucker said, tying his Penny Hardaway basketball sneakers.

Closing the briefcase, Chico walked back inside the house. Moments later he walked back out with a basketball.

"Are you ready," he asked Tucker.

"I'm ready," Tucker said, with a slight smile on his face. "Are you ready, Jordan?"

"Yes, Chico, more ready than I have ever been in my life," I said.

Everyone then walked over to the basketball court. Sid and Ruiz remained standing there pointing their guns. And with his gun in his hand, Chico sat on the bench.

Mia stood there still crying for sympathy, but no one paid her any mind. This was between men. This is what Chico wanted and had been waiting for, a game where Tucker was playing to save his and Mia's lives. And I was playing for Pedro's death—and Chico's revenge.

Chapter 20

As the two of us stood at the top of key on the basketball court, I looked over at Chico who was sitting on the bench with a tear falling down his face. The sky was beginning to darken as the night was approaching. Ruiz then cut on the light that lit up the entire basketball court for us to play.

"Best two out of three," Tucker said, stretching his arms over his head.

"Best two out of three, that's it, each game to ten," Chico said, throwing the basketball at Tucker.

"Who's ball first?" Tucker asked.

"Yours, you're the guest," Chico said.

Passing me the ball for a quick check, I passed it back and the game began.

With a quick pump fake that caught me off guard, Tucker went around me and dunked the ball.

Mia's tears stopped and a slight smile entered her face.

After getting me with another pump fake, Tucker drove to the left this time and dunked the ball again, this time with his left hand.

"Two nothing, buddy. I know you're better than that," he

smiled.

After about fifteen minutes of intense and physical play, Tucker had finally won. The final score was ten to five. Chico remained calm and relaxed sitting on the bench. Nice game, Tucker. One more and you can walk away. You and this bitch," Chico said.

"Do you want first ball this game?" Tucker asked me.

"No, you won. You get first ball," I said.

After checking the ball, Tucker quickly ran past me, threw the ball off the backboard and in mid air grabbed the ball and reverse dunked it. Even I was impressed.

"Damn!" I said, "You're faster than I thought."

"You sure your name is Jordan?" Tucker smiled, winking his eye at Mia.

Mia continued to smile. Only nine more points and they were scot-free.

After going back and forth, basket for basket, the score was nine to nine. Tucker had the ball dribbling in the corner. When he went to shoot, I stripped the ball from his hands and laid it up. Game two, 10-9, my way. Mia stopped smiling.

"Nice strip," Tucker said, sweating heavy from his head.

"I know you're not sweating already, big boy?"

"It's my ball now," I said, looking at Chico finally showing a smile on his face.

"Jordan, it's time to play now," Chico yelled from the bench.

Looking over at Chico, he winked his eye.

"Check ball," I said, passing Tucker the basketball.

Passing the ball back to me, I took a step back behind the key and shot the ball. *Swishhh!* All net!

"Nice shot. I didn't know you had a jump shot," Tucker

said.

"I just didn't shoot it. One nothing," I said.

After checking the ball again, I dribbled it through my legs, fake left, stopped and smoothly released the ball. *Swishhh!* All net again!

Sid and Ruiz stood there both smiling. Mia stood there crying. Chico sat on the bench laughing.

"Two nothing, big boy, remember your life is on the line," I said, taking the ball back out. The sweat was now pouring heavy down Tucker's face.

After another five straight, all net jump shots, the score was now 7-0.

"Tucker, can you make a damn point?" Mia yelled out.

Tucker said nothing as he passed the ball to me for a check.

Grabbing the ball, I pumped fake a jump shot, getting Tucker off his feet. Going around him, I two-hand slammed the ball. "I can dunk too. 8-0," I said, passing him the ball.

After another long jump shot from the top of the key, the score was now 9 to zip. Looking into Tucker's eyes, I could see a man who was loudly hearing the voices of death calling him. And there was no way to mute the sound. Dribbling the ball, Tucker was all over me like white on rice. Stopping at the free throw line, I stopped and let the ball smoothly roll off my fingers, headed towards the empty net.

Tucker didn't even look back to see if it went in. He didn't have to because he heard it. *Swishhh.* All net! I just walked away.

Falling to his knees in embarrassment and fear for his life, "You set me up! You set me up, Chico!" he said, in an angry voice.

Standing up now, Chico walked over and stood in front of

the terrified and scared man.

"Just like you did my brother, but he never had a chance, *did* he?"

"Chico, please, it was all Mia's idea!" he yelled.

"*Please*, Chico, let me play one more game, just *one* more game."

"The game is over!" Chico said. Pointing the Beretta at Tucker's head he unloaded the entire clip into his face. Death was instant as Tucker's tired body slumped to the ground.

"*Ahhhhhhh*," Mia screamed. "Chico, please! Please don't kill me! I'm sorry! Please, Chico! He made me do it!" Mia begged.

Chico then looked into Mia's desperate eyes and peacefully quoted a verse from the bible:

"Proverbs 5:11-12

At the end of your life you will groan,

When your flesh and body are spent.

You will say, "How I hated discipline!

How my heart spurned correction!"

"Chico, I'm sorry! Please! Please! Spare my life," Mia continued to cry out.

"Take her down to the basement. And his body too," Chico said, walking into the house.

Sid quickly grabbed Mia putting his hand over her mouth. Ruiz and I grabbed Tucker's deceased body, leaving a trail of blood behind us. Going through the garage, we went through a door and down a flight of stairs. A wooden table was in the middle of the floor. All kinds of tools were neatly hanging from the walls. While Sid continued to tightly hold the squirming Mia, Chico walked down the stairs.

"Lay her on the table and tie her up," Chico said. Ruiz and

I dropped Tucker's corpse on the concrete ground, and Ruiz grabbed Mia's legs. Chico took a thick roll of duct tape and some rope from off the wall and passed it to Sid.

Ruiz taped Mia's mouth closed and tied her body to the table then walked inside a small closet. He walked out moments later wearing a pair of goggles and carrying a chainsaw in his hand. I remained silent and took a step behind Chico. Chico nodded Ruiz, giving him the approval to begin. Pulling the string from the chainsaw, it quickly came on.

With a death look on Mia's face, she tried her best to break free. But the tight ropes would not give. Her beauty, which had always gotten her over, could no longer save her as Ruiz walked over to Mia, as she lay strapped to the table. I turned my head as he began to slice away at her once precious body. I could hear the loud sound of the chainsaw rip through her delicate flesh. Chico and Sid both stood there calm.

Finally, Ruiz stopped as Mia's mangled and torn apart body laid on the bloody table.

"Bag her up. Get that no-good piece of shit next," he said, pointing at Tucker's dead body. "Then bag him up too, and wash this place down with the hose. I'll be by your truck waiting, Sid."

Chico then walked back upstairs with me following right behind him. Chico and I sat waiting by Sid's large Tahoe truck. Chico then opened up the back.

Neither of us said a word as we both waited for Ruiz and Sid to bring up the two large bags of chopped human flesh. Forty-five minutes later...walking up the stairs, holding the extra large green plastic bags in their arms, Ruiz and Sid placed both bags inside of Sid's truck. Then Chico shut the door.

"Ruiz, get in Tucker's Range Rover and follow us.

Jordan, you follow us in Mia's Lexus," he said, throwing me the keys.

Sid and Chico got into his truck and pulled out of the large garage. Ruiz and I both followed them.

A few hundred feet from shore, the yacht calmly floated in the middle of the Pacific Ocean. The four of us each stood around by the boat's deck. The sky was pitch black. Only the stars were shining their lights down on us.

Back at shore, Mia and Tucker's cars were both parked side by side where the two of them would remain.

The two large bags with cut up pieces of human flesh both laid by Chico's feet. Pulling out a gold cross from his pocket, Chico held it to the dark sky. "God, forgive me for all of my sins. Only you know the pain of a grieving brother. Only you can judge me."

Chico then kissed the cross and threw it into the waters of the Pacific Ocean. Sid then grabbed one of the bags and opened it up releasing its foul smell into the wind. Ruiz did the same with the other bag.

Kneeling at the deck of the yacht, Sid dumped the butchered flesh into the ocean. Then he dumped the other bag as well. It wasn't long afterwards that a large swarm of man-eating sharks surrounded the yacht, aggressively fighting over the unexpected meal. Sid then grabbed the boat's hose and washed the blood from the deck. Afterwards we all went back downstairs in the yacht where Ruiz escorted us back to shore.

Sitting in a chair with a lost look on his face, Chico put his head down. Then suddenly he stood up and looked at me. "Jordan," he said.

"Yeah, Chico, what's up?"

"That's how you feed snakes to the sharks." He then sat back in his chair and closed his eyes.

The next day, Ruiz had cleaned up and destroyed anything that would connect any of us with the disappearance of Mia or Tucker's bodies. Every photo of Mia was burned and thrown away.

Inside the living room, the four of us sat around the table. After separating the money, three million dollars laid in front of each man.

"Thank you, my friends. This is y'all rewards," Chico said.

All I could think about was how a year earlier I was working at Dunkin' Donuts being accused of stealing a hundred dollars. Now, just like that, I had enough money for my family and me to be set for the rest of our lives.

I already had my own money safely put away in the security of my mother's home. Soon this three million would be joining the rest. A million dollars of it would go to my Uncle Paul to buy up some real estate around the city. Mom taught me that. She would always say, "Make your money work for you." For all the days of pain and heartache my family had seen, I promised to make sure now that they would have twice as many good days. One day, I just sat back and thought about life and everything that it has to offer. In reality, if you took all the money and material items away, I believe life would be so much better—what's more important than family? Or what's more important than love? And happiness. *Nothing*! Not all the money in the world can cure a grieving heart. Or a lonely soul! This cruel world has manipulated us to believe that money is its ruler when everyone knows that the love of money is actually the root to *all* evil. God doesn't look into your pockets. He looks into your heart. Yes, money can buy us all the most extravagant gifts in the world, but if I had to give it all up for a happy and loving family, I would be a broke man. Remember the saying, *Life's a bitch and then you die*. Well, that was wrong. Life *ain't* a bitch. Life is a pimp—a no-good ass pimp, manipulating each one of us with its charm and smooth ways. Now you know, life ain't no bitch. It never was. Life is a pimp, and then you die. We have just been mislead....

Chapter 21

Tuesday afternoon, walking into my apartment, I was finally happy to be back home. Hearing me walk through the door, Barbara rushed into my arms crying. I could tell she had missed me, but I had missed her just the same. The tears rolled down her face, as she laid cuddled in my protective arms.

"I miss you, Jordan," she said, in the most sincere voice.

"I miss you too," I said back.

"Why are you crying?" I asked.

"I think you should sit down, I have something to tell you."

"Tell me, what is it?"

"Jordan, I'm pregnant with your child." Barbara said.

"What!"

"Yesterday morning, I took a home pregnancy test and it showed positive, the only person I told was your mother. I'm just over a week. My period never came on this weekend like it was supposed to."

"It's mine?"

"What!"

"Yes, Jordan. I never slept with any man but you without

a condom on. I'm so sorry," Barbara said.

"Why are you sorry," I said, looking into her beautiful watery eyes.

"I don't want you to think I'm trying to trap you or anything. It just happened. If you want me to, I'll get rid of it."

"Barbara, look into my eyes," I said.

With a flow of running tears falling down her face, she looked into my eyes.

"I want you to have our child because it's what God wants. Sometimes things happen for a reason and I believe we were both put in each other's lives to fulfill each other's voids."

"I love you, Jordan," she said, laying her head on my shoulder. "I truly love you with all of my heart," she nervously said, shaking in my arms.

At that moment I thought about what really mattered in my life, and family was first. Then I thought about what my mom said when she told me, "Don't run away." As Barbara continued to cry on my shoulder, I whispered into her ear. "Everything will be okay. I love you too."

That evening, Uncle Paul and I were sitting inside my Mercedes outside of his apartment talking. I had just gotten finished telling him all about what had happened in L.A. For a minute I thought he might throw up in my car after hearing about the gruesome butchering of Mia and Tucker's bodies.

I then reached into the back seat of my car and grabbed a brown briefcase.

"What's this?" Uncle Paul said, as I put it on his lap.

"Open it up and see," I said smiling.

Uncle Paul then opened the briefcase. "Whoa! How much is this?"

"It's a million dollars."

"What do you want me to do with this, Jordan?"

"I want you to buy some property for our family's future."

"Okay, but next time, don't you be driving around with all this money in the car."

"I'm not worried about anybody. I keep one on the hip and the other one in the whip and pointed to the glove compartment, just like you taught me."

"What about business? We've been down for a minute."

"Oh, things will be back the same next week. The arcades will be playing once again. Chico just wanted to take a little break. He's still dealing with Pedro's death and all that has happened recently. Oh, yeah, you're going to be another uncle."

"What! Who? No... no... not Barbara..."

"Yup. She found out yesterday at the clinic."

"Is it yours?"

"I'm pretty sure it's mine, one hundred percent."

"Congratulations, Jordan."

"Thanks, Uncle Paul," I said, as he opened the door, getting out of the car holding the briefcase in his hand. "I'm going to go put this up."

"Okay," I said, "I'll talk to you tomorrow," I said as he shut the door and walked into his apartment. Once he was inside, I drove away.

Later that night...

"Hey, what's up, buddy?" I said walking into Marquise's room, sitting next to him on his bed.

"Daddy, Daddy, you're home," he said, giving me a big hug.

"Why aren't you asleep like Sharrod?"

"Grand mom said that you were coming over, so I waited."

"You waited up for me?"

"Yup!"

"Well, it's pretty late. It's way past your bedtime."

"I know, but I missed you, Daddy. I just wanted to see you."

"Did you have fun this weekend?"

"Yes, I had fun over your house. Aunt Barbara took me and Sharrod everywhere."

"Where did y'all go?"

"We went to McDonald's and to the playground and played basketball."

"You know how to play basketball?"

"Yeah, Dad, my mommy always played basketball with me. She told me it was your favorite sport."

"She did?"

"Yeah, it's mine too."

At that moment, my face had the biggest smile on it.

"Are you any good?"

"I can dunk on my little court that Grand mom bought me."

"You can?"

"Yup! And I can beat Sharrod playing too."

"One day, I'm going to come play with you. Right now it's getting late. Give me a hug and get ready for bed, for school tomorrow."

After giving me a hug, I stood up and walked to the door.

"Daddy, I love you," he said.

"I love you too, Marquise," I said, as I turned out his light and shut the door.

"What's up, big bro," Shawn said, rushing into his bedroom holding the telephone.

"What's going on, Shawn?" I said.

Putting the phone down to his chest, "My new girl-friend," he whispered, as he quickly shut his bedroom door.

As I walked down the long hall and went down stairs, I noticed my mom sitting all alone on the couch. The music on the stereo system was quietly playing Patti Labelle's *If Only You Knew*, from out of the clear Bose speakers that were each on opposite sides of the living room. My mom was probably Patti Labelle's biggest fan. Ever since I could remember, only three female singers my mom would always be listening to. Aretha Franklin and Teena Marie were the others, but none more than the soulful and beautiful voice of Patti Labelle. Taking a seat next to her on the couch, I interrupted her zone.

"Hey, boy, you scared me," she said, opening her eyes.

"I'm sorry, Mom," I said, with a smile on my face.

"I put that money up that you asked me to. It's in your safe with the rest."

"Thanks, Mom."

"Did you talk to Barbara?" she asked.

"Yes, we talked today."

"How do you feel about her being pregnant?"

"I really didn't think about it."

"Well, I can assure you of one thing. That she's very afraid."

"Afraid of what?"

"She's afraid of losing you. That woman has been hurt so many times and now she's found someone special in her life. It's been a long time since she's loved a man. She wasn't ever going to tell you that she was pregnant. I made her. She was just going to get an abortion and never let you know, but I convinced her to let you have a say-so. One thing for sure, a woman like that would never hurt you. Or ever leave your side."

"Well I told her I want her to keep it."

"I knew you would," my mother said smiling.

"You knew?"

"I know my child. How's Chico doing?" she said, changing the subject.

"He's holding up."

"Did y'all two handle y'all business?"

"Yeah, we took care of everything."

"Good, now you'll be home for a while. Marquise would love that."

"Yeah, he and I are going out for his birthday Thursday. He wants me to take him by his mother's grave."

"He does?"

"Yeah, he asked me the other day. I told him that I would."

"I think that's a good idea. He told me that he had something to tell her."

"He told you that too?"

"Yeah, he said he had to tell her something important."

"You can come get him on Thursday morning. I told him he didn't have to go to school on his birthday."

"I'll pick him up early then."

I then stood up and walked to the door as my mom laid back and finished listening to her Patti Labelle CD.

Before I walked out, I paused and turned back around. "Hey, Mom," I said, standing with the door now opened.

"Yes, what is it, Jordan?"

"Thanks."

"Thanks for what?" she said smiling.

"For everything," I said, walking out the front door.

Driving on the expressway back to my apartment, I couldn't help but think of Barbara being pregnant. I had always thought that Cookie and I would have at least three or four kids running around the house playing. It never entered my mind, ever, having a child with someone else besides her. But the more I thought about becoming a father again, the happier I felt inside. Barbara was a good woman—a woman that I had cared for very much. A woman who I believed had paid her dues and deserved happiness. And one I looked forward to spending the rest of my life with.

Chapter 22

April 9th...

After waking up early on this Thursday morning, I took a shower and got dressed. Barbara was still in bed sleeping when I kissed her on her cheek waking her up. "Hey baby," I said. "Where are you going so early."

"Today's Marquise's birthday, remember". "Oh, that's right, I bet he's waiting". Barbara smilingly said. "Yeah, I'm pretty sure he is". "I want you to know that I really love the relationship between you and Marquise". "Thank you Barbara, I just want to be the best father that I could be". "You're a wonderful father, that's why I love you", Barbara said, sitting up giving me a warm hug.

Twenty minutes later...I arrived at my mother's home where Marquise was up already, looking out the window when I pulled infront of the door. Dressed in a outfit that his mother had bought him for Christmas, the first thing I noticed was the small gold chain around his neck that said, *Never Cry*. "What's up daddy"?

"What's up, buddy?" I said, walking through the door,

giving him a hug. "Happy birthday. You're a big boy now."

"Thanks, Dad," he said, smiling.

"Where's your grand mom?"

"She went back to bed after she got me washed and dressed."

"Are you ready," I said.

"Yes, Daddy, I'm ready to go see my mommy," he said, rushing out the door.

After getting inside the car, we drove off headed for the Glory of God cemetery in Mt. Erie where Cookie's body was laid to rest.

Lying in bed, Barbara heard her cell phone ringing and got up and answered it. "Hello," she said, still half asleep.

"Hey, Barbara, it's me."

"What's up, Steve?"

"Where are you?"

"I'm over a friend's house."

"Is he paying," Steve said, laughing into the phone.

"It's a she. What's up, Steve?" Barbara said in a serious voice.

"We're back in business tomorrow. I found a new man to take RW's place. I wanted to wait till Friday to introduce him to you and the rest of the girls."

"Okay, I'll let them know. Tomorrow is fine."

"Why didn't you tell me you moved out of your apartment?"

"How do you know?"

"I drove by there yesterday. Where are you staying now?"

"Still at my sister's house in South Philly."

"Next time let me know when you decide to move somewhere."

"I will. I'll call you later Steve. I'm still half asleep."

"No, don't call me on my cell phone. I've been using pay-phones."

"Why?"

"It's been cutting on and off for some reason. I think it might be tapped. I'll just call you tomorrow."

"Okay, bye Steve," Barbara said, switchin' off the phone.

She got back into bed and went back to sleep.

The sun was shining all over on this beautiful day. The wind was barely blowing as Marquise and I walked through this community of dead bodies. Besides us, only the flying birds and running squirrels were inside this final resting place for human life. Looking around at the different tombstones made me think about all the friend that I had lost and all the men and women who lost their lives on the streets of Philadelphia. As Marquise and I walked through the cemetery, we finally approached his mother's tombstone. Piles of different colored roses lay all around Cookie's grave. I had paid and gotten them delivered the day before. I couldn't help but shed a tear as I read the words on the tombstone. *In our darkest skies you remain that bright star that shines forever, In memory of...Carolyn 'Cookie' Palmer. Sunrise 1975—Sunset 1998.*

"Daddy, don't cry," Marquise said, looking into my watery eyes. "Daddy, can you go over there for a minute and let me tell my mommy something," he said, as he got on his knees in front of her tombstone.

Walking a few feet away, I stood there and watched him as he whispered into his mother's tombstone. I still couldn't believe how he had grown up so fast.

"Okay, Daddy," he said, standing up. "I'm ready to go."

With a smile on his face, he grabbed my hand and the two of us walked back to the car.

For the rest of the day, Marquise and I enjoyed our time together. After going to a movie and getting something to eat at his favorite restaurant ... McDonalds, I went to the toy store and bought him that new bike that he wanted for his birthday. Boxed neatly in the trunk, he couldn't wait till I put it together so he could ride it. I also picked up a few board games so he and Sharrod could play together.

After taking him shopping downtown at the Gallery Mall, we both had a seafood dinner at Red Lobster. The sky was beginning to darken as I drove down the crowded Broad Street. Turning down on a side street to avoid all the traffic I stopped at a red light.

"Daddy! Daddy! There goes Steve!" Marquise shouted as he was pointing his finger at the glass. "He's right there!"

Looking through my car's tinted window, I noticed Steve talking on a payphone a few feet away from his double-parked Lexus. Quickly, I pulled behind his car while he paid me no mind and continued to go on with his conversation. With my loaded 9-millimeter on my hip, I rushed out of the car.

"Yo, buddy," I said, walking up a few feet behind Steve.

"Hold on one minute, I'll be right off," he said. "Hey, don't I know you from somewhere?" he said, turning around, with one hand still holding the phone and the other inside his jacket. "Your face looks familiar," he said, dropping the phone.

"It should, I'm Cookie's baby's father," I said, slowly reaching under my shirt to grab my 9-millimeter.

"Oh, shit! I remember you now," he said, pulling out the

black Glock from his jacket pocket that he already had gripped in his hand.

With my gun in my hand and Steve's already cocked and pointed at my head—three loud gunshots went off.

I noticed Steve's body slumping in front of the payphone.

Looking over my shoulder, Marquise was standing there holding my other 9-millimeter with both hands.

"Marquise! Oh, my God!" I yelled. "Oh, my God!"

"I got him, Daddy! I got him for my mommy!" he said.

"Get in the car, Marquise! Hurry up," I said, as he quickly got in and shut the door. Rushing to the car, I jumped in and quickly sped off.

"Give me that gun, Marquise," I said, putting both back into the opened glove compartment.

"Daddy, I'm sorry," he said with a flow of tears now falling down his face. "But I promised my mommy."

"You promised your mom what Marquise! What are you talking about?" I said, nervously looking through the rearview mirror.

"I promised my mommy that I would get the bad man who killed her. That's what I wanted to tell her."

"I don't believe this," I said, driving down the dark street.

Back at the payphone, still barely alive from the three gunshots in his chest, Steve laid inside of a policeman's arms coughing and shaking inside a large pool of his own blood.

"Marquise little... Marquise little..."

"Everything will be okay. The ambulance is on its way," the officer said.

"Marquise little... Marquise little..." Steve said as both his eyes finally closed with him dying in the policeman's arms.

Back inside the car...

"Don't say anything to anybody, Marquise! Nobody! You hear me?"

"I won't, Daddy, I won't tell anybody."

"Not one word!"

"I promise, Daddy, I won't tell anybody."

"I don't believe this shit!" I said, as I continued to drive Marquise back home. I just couldn't believe Marquise had shot Steve.

After taking Marquise back home, I went to my Uncle Paul's house and told him what had happened. After getting rid of the guns, we both came back to his apartment where we both nervously sat and watched the 11 o'clock news.

"This evening on the corner of Seventeenth and Cumberland, a young man was shot down while talking on a payphone. Steven Young of North Philadelphia was found still alive when Officer Gordon Lewis arrived at the scene. Moments later, in Officer Lewis' arm, the thirty-one-year-old died a few feet away from his running Lexus. Witnesses told police that two men were seen fleeing from the scene in a black Mercedes. Both men appeared to have been in their mid-twenty's with one at least six feet and the other around five feet."

Uncle Paul turned off the TV. "You got to put the car up for a while," he said.

"Alright. What else?"

"Call and tell Barbara you have an emergency and have to go away for a few days."

"Okay. You think I should go to California?"

"No. If they found out anything, they'll check and see that

you ran. That will help incriminate you. Just chill. You're going to stay here for a few days and just wait. Plus, we don't need Chico getting involved. He's got his own problems."

"You're right. I'll just chill here."

After calling Barbara and telling her that I would be gone for a few days, I nervously laid back on my Uncle's couch and feel asleep.

Chapter 23

I stayed over my uncle's for a few days till things had calmed down, watching the news all day to see if any new information had been found on the murder of Steve. The news reporters said the same thing. That no one had been arrested and no further leads had been reported.

I had asked my mother how Marquise was doing and she told me that he was doing fine and actually seemed happier for some reason.

Barbara had seen everything on the news and front page of the newspaper. She still had no idea what had happened and what was going on. Only three people knew what had happened on that night—me, Uncle Paul and Marquise.

Monday, April 13th...

Inside my uncle's Ford Expedition, I pulled into the parking lot of my apartment complex. Everything seemed normal as I looked all around. Standing in the doorway, Barbara saw me when I pulled up and got inside.

"Hi, baby," she said, kissing me on my cheek.

As I started to pull off, a swarm of cars quickly surrounded us.

"Police! Get out of the car! Get the fuck out of the car!" I heard, as undercover police officers all stood behind their cars pointing loaded guns at the two of us. "Get out of the car!" they continued to say.

We both stayed calm as we each opened our door with our hands up in the air.

"Get on the ground!" a voice yelled out.

Lying on the ground, I could feel the cold steel handcuffs quickly wrap around my wrist. "Jordan Marquise Henderson, you are under arrest for the murder of Steven Young," a cop said, helping me to my feet.

Looking over at the tearful Barbara, I noticed she wasn't handcuffed. They had gotten who they wanted…me. After reading me my rights, I was taken to a waiting car. Before I got inside, "Call Uncle Paul. Tell him to get me a lawyer," I said, as the officer pushed my head into the car. Watching Barbara run through the door, the car quickly pulled off.

April 14th…

The next day, as I laid inside my cell on the cold steel cot inside the Philadelphia police headquarters at Eight and Race Streets, Chico and Uncle Paul were waiting in the lobby as my lawyer came to talk to me. A short Italian man in his mid-40's was let in holding a large briefcase and a cell phone in his other hand.

"Hi, my name is John Martelli," he said, shaking my hand.

"Hey, aren't you the guy who won that case for the mob?"

"Yeah, I help beat the bodies; they were still charged with racketeering."

"What do you think, Mr. Martelli?" I said.

"It doesn't look good, Mr. Henderson."

"Call me Jordan," I said, standing up, pacing around my cell.

"They have witnesses who say they saw your car at the scene and two men quickly driving away. I also recently found out that the gun that Mr. Young was found with at the time was the same gun used in the murder of two prostitutes, one being a Miss Carolyn Palmer, your child's mother. Neighbors at Miss Palmer's last known residence told police that you were seen driving around the neighborhood and that you and Miss Palmer had a big argument one day and you took your son away.

They also are investigating the murder of a Rodney "Rock" Walters who was murdered a few weeks ago and was believed to be a friend of Mr. Young. I was told that the two of you were both in the same prison at the same time, but the most vital information was from Mr. Young himself who repeatedly called your name before finally dying in the officer's arms.

"This does not look good at all. The prosecutor will surely convince a jury of first degree premeditated murder and ask for the death penalty. There's just too much evidence against you, Jordan. Too much!"

"Well, what do you think I should do?"

"I do not bullshit my clients around and I do not like to lose cases, but this is one I honestly can't see winning. It would almost take a miracle to win this case. I think you should plead out and take life, if I can convince the prosecutor we won't take it to trial. You think about it. I've got a lot of paperwork to do. I'll be back tomorrow for your answer," Mr. Martelli said and she shook my hand and walked away.

Sitting on my cot, my head seemed like it had spun a thousand times. All I could think about were two things—life and death.

After my mother and Barbara visited me earlier that day, Chico was my last visit for the evening. Inside the visiting room, the two of us were talking.

"I don't know what to say, Jordan. It's really up to you. I'd rather have you alive though. Damn! Jordan. Whatever you decide, I'll be there by your side, homey, even if I got to go get Johnny Cochran myself. You should have controlled your temper and done things like we planned."

"Chico, I didn't kill 'im."

"What!!!"

"You heard me. I didn't kill 'im."

"Well, who did it then?"

"My son," I whispered.

"Marquise?!!!"

"Yes, Marquise *killed* him," I whispered again.

"Oh, shit! Oh, this is bad, Jordan."

"That's why I got to plead out and take life. I got to do it for my son or they will take him from me until he turns eighteen. No one knows but my Uncle Paul and now you."

"Damn! Damn! Damn!" Chico said, putting his head down.

"I'm telling my lawyer to get me a deal. I'm pleading out before these people start finding out other shit, you know what I mean."

Looking up at me, with a set of teary eyes, Chico agreeably shook his head.

"Don't worry, Chico, about me. You just make sure my family's alright."

"I will, Jordan. Everything will be taken care of, I promise."

"I know it will. I know I can count on you, my brother."

Once Chico's hour visitation was over, I was taken back to my single cell. Lying on my cold cot that night, I thought about everything, how my life had changed once again. How I would once again be separated from my child. And my new baby that was on the way. Still deep down inside, I knew I was doing the right thing. I would rather die before I would cause any harm to my child. He still had his whole life ahead of him. Mine had come and gone. I had lived the life I always wanted, the money and cars and women. I had known what this cruel world was about. I never thought that I would one day be back behind bars. I had already given these people *six* years. Now they would have the rest of what they've probably been waiting for. Another black male, caught up in the harsh life of the streets. I thought about Barbara and my mother. And how we constantly weakened the strength of our families, the women. They are the ones who feel this pain we have. They are the ones who always suffer most. Still, they remain by our sides as we slowly drain every bit of remaining strength they have left. I want all the women out there to know that we truly love y'all. If only you knew that this is bigger than us. We really have no control over our destiny. All I can pray for now is that my son doesn't follow in these same fatal footsteps, which is usually the case when a child grows up with no parents. But with my mom and Barbara around, at least he has a better chance than me to make it. Since my first breath, I began dying, literally. You could never understand my pain, unless you've walked my same deadly path. Like so many others, the ghetto has been my downfall. The bad part about it is, there's no escape. We can leave the ghetto, but the ghetto will never leave us. We can run away, but it will soon find us. It will search us out till there is nowhere else to run or hide.

April 17th...

A few days later, my lawyer and the prosecutor all sat inside a small room inside the police headquarters building. The prosecutor was a female named Candise Abraham. Mrs. Abraham was known for her hard commitment to clean up the deadly streets of Philadelphia. With her long blond hair, she stood around five-eight. An attractive woman in her mid-thirty's, Mrs. Abraham had been Philly's top prosecutor for five years.

"I would like to have a talk with Mr. Henderson alone," she said.

"Candise, I don't think that would be appropriate," Mr. Martelli said.

"I'll talk to her," I said, sitting across the table from her.

"We are willing to accept the deal, there is not too much more to discuss," he said.

"Martelli, can I *please* just have a word with Mr. Henderson?"

"It's okay, John. I'll talk to her," I said.

Getting up from his seat, "I'll be in the hallway," he said.

"Yes, what is it, Mrs. Abraham?"

"Mr. Henderson..."

"Can you call me Jordan, please?"

Looking at me, she smiled. "Okay, Jordan. I have been looking over this whole case for the last few days. I have studied this entire case and it becomes more and more strange as I go on. I have read police reports and witness reports and things just do not add up."

"What *do* you mean?"

"I mean, I believe you are hiding something."

"I told you I did it. That I would take the deal and plead out to life."

"I understand, but what I don't understand is why would you get the number one criminal lawyer in the city and plead out in three days? Something isn't right."

"I did it! I just didn't want to bullshit you around, that's all."

"Then why are you *bullshitting* me now?"

"What are you talking about? I'm telling the truth."

"Jordan, when I read the police report, it said that Mr. Young's final words were "Marquise little," and he repeated it until he finally died in the officer's arms.

"So what does that mean? He called out my name."

"After a few witnesses said that they saw two men leave the scene of the crime, I got suspicious. Every one of them said that one man was tall and the other was very short. Then I put two and two together. Mr. Young wasn't saying Marquise Little. He was saying little Marquise. You didn't kill Mr. Young. It was your son who did."

"I told you I did it, Mrs. Abraham. I told you it was me!"

"Let me finish. That was on his birthday. I have many reports that you were seen driving around with him that day. You were seen downtown and someone even remembered seeing you at the movie theater on Delaware Avenue."

Nervously I sat in my chair as she continued on.

"Now I understood why you wanted to plead out so fast. You're protecting your child. You'd rather do life behind bars than cause any pain to your son. I admire that, Jordan. I really do. So you know what I did when I realized what you had done?"

I remained silent as she continued.

"I did you the biggest favor in the world. I went over Mr. Young's entire criminal record, and believe me, it's as long as a mile. He had beaten two homicides one in '88 and another in '92—both women. And he was also being investigated for two recent murders, one being Miss Carolyn Palmer. Mr. Young was a very dangerous young man, the type of man that I despise. One who preys off vulnerable women.

"I then looked at your record. You served six years in prison for car theft. I looked and looked, but that was it. Car theft! On your entire criminal record, all you have is a charge for stealing automobiles.

"I then said to myself, does this man really deserve to do life in prison for something he did not do? By Mr. Young being killed, you have actually helped us solve two murders.

"For days, I thought heavy about this. I even lost sleep over it and my husband hates when I don't tuck him in at night," she said, smiling. "Then I said, what the hell! He did *me* a favor; I'll do him a favor. I will not charge you or accept a plea of life from you, Jordan."

"You won't?"

"No. I won't even charge you with second or third degree either."

"You *won't?*"

"Nope. I'm offering you a deal right now for seven years for manslaughter."

"What! Seven years, that's *it?*"

"That's it! Seven years, for manslaughter."

"I'll take it!" I said, standing up from my seat smiling.

Mrs. Abraham then stood up from her chair and shook my

hand. "Promise me one thing, Jordan," she said, folding her briefcase up and walking to the door.

"You name it!" I said, still in a state of shock.

"That you'll keep those guns out of your child's hands."

I stood there silent. I knew it was a trick question she asked.

"I'm waiting," she said, smiling at me.

"I promise," I said, sitting back in my chair.

"I'll tell your lawyer. You take care, Jordan and stay out of trouble."

I just sat there shaking my head. God had answered my prayers. I could do ten, I said to myself!"

My lawyer then walked back into the room. "What went on? What happened? How did you pull this off?" were some of the questions he asked.

Looking into my lawyer's happy face, "It wasn't me, Mr. Martelli, it was destiny," I said. "It was *destiny*."

Chapter 24

Two years later... 2000

Sitting in my cell, I was waiting for my family to show up. Every weekend my mother, my new bride and our three children would come visit me. Marquise was now ten years old and almost as tall as me. Uncle Paul and Chico said he was going to be one helluva basketball player. Even better than I was. They both made sure he kept a basketball in his hand. But more importantly, his head in the books. Barbara and I had gotten married on Valentine's day 1999 in a nice ceremony inside the prison chapel.

On December 18, my birthday, my daughter Carolyn Amini Henderson, was born, six pounds five ounces. My younger brother Shawn even became the top student in his class, earning honors and getting scholarship offers from some of the top colleges in the country. My mom had bought two more bars and now had five all together around the city. Uncle Paul bought some apartment buildings and rented them out cheaply to Section-8 approved families. Chico would fly from California every month and visit me for the whole weekend. He eventually got engaged to some twin he met at a party I recall. As for me, all I could do was take it one day at a time. Once I return home, nothing would ever separate me and my family again. I was given a chance that many wish they could received. I knew from now on I had to do the right thing. Out of everything, I only regret not being there for my family. To see my daughter's first steps or Marquises first dunk, or Shawn graduate from high school, then college. But still, I couldn't complain. One day at least I would be back. At least I was given a second chance. I would have another opportunity to live out my life. And next time, things would be a whole lot different. I had learned something very important from being in this place. That nothing in life is worth more than your freedom. So once you receive your freedom back, never let it go again. Always keep your head up, and like Marquise would always say, Never cry…

Acknowledgements

First and foremost I give all my praise to God, my strength, soul and savior. Also I'd like to thank the following list of people: my mother, Belinda, my sisters, Dawn, Tammy and Tanya. My brother Sean. To my two sons-Marquise and Niguel. Thanks to all my good friends for their support and encouragement. It means a lot to me just knowing you have my back.

Wallace "Duke" Gray, and the entire Gray family. My good friend, Darrin 'Jeeky' Lockings. Robert Hennigan, Sekue Clark, Duran-Norfleet, Kenneth "Cheese" Johnson, and my entire ICH family-Colossus, Reese, Sport, Bossman, Scarfo, A-Town, Shorty-Raw, HH-Spady, Var, T. P. Dollarz, and Young Savage.

To my fans, you truly are a blessing and I thank you for your continued support. I write for you.

To all the bookstores and vendors, thank you for keeping your shelves filled with my novels. Empire Books, DC Book Diva, Black & Nobel, Street Knowledge Books, Amaiya Ent., Expressions, Divin Books In the Hood, and Xanyell and Quada, from Horizon Books; thanks for holding me down always.

To all the men and woman incarcerated in the State and Federal prison across the county, I'd like to say thank you for all your support and uplifting letters. Stay positive in your moment of darkness, as the light always shines on those who believe.

R.I. P to Man, Mark, Troy, Rob and Harold "Georgie" Johnson.

Jimmy DaSaint

DASAINT ENTERTAINMENT ORDER FORM
Ordering Books
Please visit www.dasaintentertainment.com to place online orders.
Or
You can fill out this form and send it to:

DaSaint Entertainment
PO Box 97
Bala Cynwyd, PA 19004

Title	Price	QTY
Black Scarface	$15.00	_____
Black Scarface II	$15.00	_____
Young Rich & Dangerous	$15.00	_____
What Every Woman Wants	$15.00	_____
The UnderWorld	$15.00	_____
A Rose Among Thorns	$15.00	_____
Contract Killer	$15.00	_____
On Everything I Love	$15.00	_____
Money Desires and Regrets	$15.00	_____
Ain't No Sunshine	$14.99	_____

Make Checks or Money Orders out to: DaSaint Entertainment

Name: _____

Address: _____

_____

City: _____ State:_____ Zip:_____

Telephone: _____

Email: _____

Add $3.50 for shipping and handling
$1.50 for each additional book
($4.95 for Expedited Shipping)

**Featured Author...Check Tiona Brown out at
www.tiona.net**

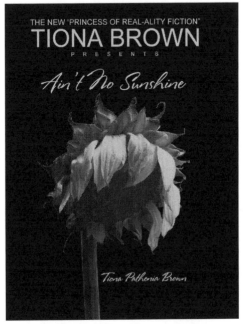

Ain't No Sunshine
A Novel By Tiona Brown

Coming Soon
Black Scarface III
The Wrath of Face

Made in the USA
Lexington, KY
14 March 2014